MW00769245

LUCK

OF THE

Devil

FORGE TRILOGY BOOK TWO

MEGHAN

MARCH

Visit my website at www.meghanmarch.com.

CONTENTS

LUCK OF THE DEVIL

.

Book Two of the Forge Trilogy

Meghan March

ABOUT THIS BOOK

My poker face has always been my greatest asset, along with my grit and determination. I was beholden to no one. Asked permission for nothing.

Then Jericho Forge took my life by storm.

I traded my freedom for something infinitely more precious, but I didn't realize Forge was holding an unbeatable hand.

Now, all I have to do is survive the high-stakes game my life has become—with my heart intact.

But not falling in love with Forge will take the luck of the devil.

Luck of the Devil is the second book of the Forge Trilogy and should be read following *Deal with the Devil.* The Forge Trilogy concludes in *Heart of the Devil.*

FORGE

Twenty-five years ago

*M*y busted arm hung limp as I sneaked through the towers of shipping containers stacked like the Legos I was stupid enough to ask Santa for when I was six. That was when Uncle Ruben had found the letter I'd written, and had laughed so hard he cried as he read off my requests.

Boots, soxs, warm coat, and Legos.
Also, can you give Uncle Ruben something good so he stops
hurting Aunt Dora?

UNCLE RUBEN'S laughter had cut off and his eyes turned mean when he got to the last part. The moment played in my mind vividly as I scooted around the corner to hide from one of the dockyard workers.

"You show anyone this?"

I'd shaken my head once before his arm swung and the back of his hand connected with my face. I'd staggered to the side and he lashed out again, this time hitting me with a closed fist that knocked me to the floor.

"Don't you ever fucking ask me for another thing. The world doesn't give shit to kids like you. You're a waste of space. Fucking worthless, just like your whore of a mother." He'd looked down at the blood pooling beneath my cheek on the linoleum Aunt Dora scrubbed weekly on her hands and knees. "Clean that shit up before I kick your fucking teeth in."

That was the first time he'd hit me, but it wasn't the last. I became his favorite punching bag after Dora was unconscious every night.

But never again.

Aunt Dora was dead. We'd put her in the ground this afternoon, and as soon as we got home, Ruben had found the bottle.

He'd cried. He'd screamed. He'd cursed God. Then he came outside to find me in the shed where I tried to stay out of his way. Now that I was fourteen, I was getting stronger, and most of the time, I was quicker than him. But not when I was cornered, and he was in the nasty, superhuman stage of drunk.

When Ruben's knuckles had crunched against my jaw, I'd sworn it would be the last time. *He will never fucking put his hands on me again.* I'd chanted that promise silently to myself as he landed hit after kick after hit.

I'd lain bleeding on the dirt floor, trying not to breathe or move, hoping he'd finally go away if I played dead. After he'd lost interest in jamming his boots into my ribs, Ruben had stumbled out of the shed and back to the house.

Afraid to move, I'd stayed there, breathing in the scent of

musty dirt and coppery blood for fifteen minutes. Then I'd stood up slowly, trying not to puke up the potluck food from the ladies at church, and grabbed the bag I'd stashed in there two weeks ago, knowing that my time was coming just like Aunt Dora's, God rest her soul.

Dora's cancer had eaten her up from the inside out, and every single day, as she got weaker, she'd begged me to run. *Save yourself, Jericho*, she'd say, but I couldn't let her die alone with Ruben. No one deserved that. Especially not my aunt. She smelled like cinnamon and gave good hugs until her arms got too weak for her to lift them.

As she'd taken her last breath, I'd held her hand and told her she was going to a better place, and I meant it. Nothing could be worse than the hell she'd endured.

Now it was time for me to do what she'd asked. *Save myself.*

I slipped my jacked-up arm through the strap of the backpack and forced down the urge to cry as my shoulder burned like someone had shoved a hot fire poker into it.

No more tears. Not ever. I wouldn't give Ruben the satisfaction.

As I tiptoed out of the shed, I took one last look at the house. All the lights were on, but no shadows moved. Ruben had to be passed out drunk by now.

More than anything, I wished I had the balls to take the gas can from the shed and light that bitch up so Ruben could roast in hell, but I couldn't. Dora wouldn't want it.

She was the only good thing that house had ever held. I didn't remember my mom, but Ruben hadn't let a day go by without telling me what a piece of shit she was for leaving me there and taking off.

Maybe she and I had something in common, because I disappeared into the darkness, and I was never going back.

With every piece of me screaming in pain, I made the

four-mile trek to the docks where Ruben worked. I knew how to sneak and where to hide in the stacks of cargo, because sometimes he used to smuggle shit out and made me help.

That's where I was right now, waiting for the security guards to get on with their shift so I could keep moving.

A beam of light cut across the row of containers, and I scooted back into the shadows.

"You see something over here, Sam?"

I didn't know the guy who spoke, but then again, it wasn't like Ruben had many friends who came over. He drank by himself.

"Nah, man. But I just saw a rat the size of my schnauzer. I swear, those fuckers are eating each other to survive now."

"Fucking nasty."

Gravel crunched as they walked away, and I prayed they kept going so I didn't have to run. I wasn't sure if my body could take it.

The guy who wasn't Sam said something into his radio about what was next up to be loaded, and the groaning metal crane came closer. "Did you stow the shit already?"

"Yeah, it's in there."

Ha. See, Uncle Ruben? You weren't the only one smuggling shit to make extra cash.

I chanced tilting my head up to watch as the claws descended toward the container I was using for cover. *Fuck.* My hiding place was about to disappear.

"Did you lock it back up? That shit needs to look perfect. No one can find it until it's unloaded, or we don't get paid."

"Goddammit. The rat distracted me before I could shut it. The lock's in my fucking pocket."

Shit. You've gotta be kidding me.

Their footsteps changed direction, and the sound of crunching gravel grew louder as they moved my way. I slunk back and spotted an unlocked door they must have been heading toward.

I had fifteen seconds, maybe ten, to make a decision.

If I ran, they'd catch me for sure, and I'd be sent back to Ruben. So really, it wasn't much of a choice to make at all.

I'm never fucking going back.

I slipped between the open doors of the container into the pitch black. Inside, it stank like rotten fruit and piss.

Using my good hand, I felt in front of me. Smooth rounded edges told me it was filled with plastic drums. With my shoulder screaming in pain, I jammed myself between two rows a second before the door slammed shut, cutting off any trace of light.

Metal scraped on metal as he locked it up, and a breath later, the container rocked as the crane latched on. As soon as it lifted off the ground, my stomach roiled again.

I'm gonna die.

The container swung in the air, and all I could picture was the crane letting go and it tumbling to the ground.

I'm gonna fucking die.

But I didn't. A few minutes later, I was no longer swinging. Metal scraped, and the container groaned as it came to a halt.

On a ship. Bound for who the fuck knows where.

I wasn't planning to stow away like this when I slipped through the fence. The candy bars and water I shoved in my bag wouldn't last me more than a week, and God only knew where the hell this thing was going or how long it would take to get there.

Which meant I might have been right. I was gonna die.

I curled my good arm around my backpack, telling myself this was better than letting Ruben beat me to death.

ALONE IN THE DARKNESS, I lost track of time. The smell of my own shit added to the stench inside the container made me too nauseated to eat.

My brain played tricks on me, showing me pictures that weren't there. People who weren't there either. I couldn't sleep without nightmares. And the heat, fuck . . . the heat.

The bottles of water I had were long gone. My kidneys hurt, and I could barely manage to piss.

I was right that first night. I was gonna die here, trapped in a metal box like a fucking animal. I should have stayed. Should have fought back. Even prison would have been better than this. My snap decision was going to be my end.

That's when I broke.

My limp arm hung to the side as I crawled toward the door I entered who knew how many days ago. With what little remaining strength I had, I curled my good hand into a fist and banged it against the metal.

"Help! Let me out! Help!"

Nothing.

I pounded until my hand went numb, and my voice faded away.

I passed out, hoping God wouldn't torture me by letting me wake up again.

———

"JESUS FUCKING CHRIST. You're telling me we've had this kid locked in a container for ten goddamned days?"

"It appears that way, Captain."

The voices roused me from sleep, and I thought I was dreaming. Surely, I had to be, because there was no hot metal beneath me, only scratchy sheets, and it smelled like antiseptic and not shit. My shoulder pain had faded to a dull ache, but my ribs still hurt like a bitch, so maybe it wasn't a dream.

"Who have you told? Who knows?" The pissed-off, gruff voice made me wonder if whoever found me was as bad or worse than Uncle Ruben.

"Just me, Tony, and the doc, Captain. We heard him and brought him right here, and then I got you."

Shit. The captain. That couldn't be good. I forced open my eyes, and blindingly bright light seared my retinas. I winced and slammed them shut.

"Hey, kid. Can you hear us? Open your eyes." It was the captain's gruff voice.

"Too bright," I mumbled, and my raw throat made me pay for both words.

"Fuck. I didn't think about that. Doc, kill the overhead lights. The kid's been living in the dark for over a week."

From behind my closed lids, I could tell when the lights dimmed.

"Try now. Shouldn't kill you."

I squinted, and when the brightness didn't cause me pain, I opened my eyes a little further.

Above me, two men hovered. One wore navy-blue coveralls, and the other had on a white button-down and a navy tie. It didn't take a genius to figure out which was the captain. He looked older than Uncle Ruben, with his dark beard going gray, but he was tall and broad and didn't have a hint of my uncle's beer gut.

"Good to see you're awake, kid. You want to tell me how the fuck you ended up on my ship?"

"Water," I croaked out.

"Doc," the captain barked.

A blond man wearing a white coat came to the side of the bed with a clear plastic cup and held a straw to my lips. "Don't drink too fast, kid," he said, but I sucked down the cool, crisp liquid as fast as I could. "Hold up. You'll puke if you drink too much." He pulled it away before I was done.

"So, what do we do with him now?" the captain asked the doctor like I wasn't even there.

"He's got IV fluids going. He's massively dehydrated, as you'd expect. His shoulder was dislocated, but I relocated it while he was out. Kinder that way. His torso is covered with healing contusions, and if I had to guess, I'd say he likely has bruised or broken ribs."

"Am I gonna die?" The words felt like they were drawn from my throat by rusty pliers.

The doctor shook his head. "You're lucky as hell we found you when we did. A few more days without water . . ." He trailed off, but I knew what he was going to say.

I would have died.

"What the fuck do we do with him?" the man in coveralls asked.

"Report him to the authorities in Baltimore," the captain said. "They'll have to track down his parents, and we'll put him on a plane home."

"No." I coughed twice, and my ribs protested. "Please. Don't."

The captain looked down at me, his brown eyes scanning my face. From the way the man studied me, the remains of Uncle Ruben's handiwork were still visible.

"Give me one good reason, kid. I could lose my license if I don't. My whole fucking business."

"He'll kill me if you send me back."

The captain crouched by the side of the cot. "Who will kill you?"

I coughed again, trying to clear my throat. "My uncle. I won't go back. Fucking ever. I don't care what you do to me. I'll never go back there."

The captain glanced up at the doctor before looking back down at me. "He beat on you a lot?"

My pride reared up, but a voice in my head told me to tell

him the truth, at least about this. "As often as he could. He's a mean drunk."

"You have no other family?"

"No, sir. My aunt died the day I left. That's when he busted my shoulder."

The captain's dark eyebrows knit together, and white lines appeared in the weathered skin around his eyes and mouth. "How old are you, kid?"

My brain was slowly coming back to life, and something told me if I gave him my real age, he'd get me off this boat faster than I could finish answering his questions.

"Seventeen. Almost eighteen. I can work. I work hard. Just give me a chance. I swear, I won't fuck it up."

Once again, his gaze flicked to the doctor and the guy in the coveralls. "Everyone out. Don't say a fucking thing about this, or I'll toss you overboard."

The two men nodded, and they filed out of the room. When we were alone, the captain pulled up a chair and sat down beside my cot.

"How old are you really, kid?"

"I told you—"

"No, you *lied* to me."

I pressed my chapped, peeling lips together. "You can't send me back. I won't go. I'll run again. I don't care where."

"Then tell me the truth. How old are you?"

I released a long breath and crumpled the white sheet in my fist. "Fourteen. Almost fifteen. But I'm smart. I'm strong. I can work. I'll outwork every man you have on this boat. I swear to Christ. Just give me a chance."

"You should be in school. A cargo ship is no place for a kid," the captain replied, crushing my hope that he'd let me stay.

"What about cabin boys? Don't they have a place on a ship? I can do that. Whatever you need. Scrub floors. I'm good at cleaning. I can work in the kitchen. Do whatever. Please, just don't send me back."

The captain rose and dragged a hand through his salt-and-pepper hair. "What's your name, kid?"

"Jericho Forge."

"You got balls, Jericho Forge. I'll give you that." His jaw shifted, and I knew he was considering what might end up being my death sentence.

"Please, just give me a chance, sir. I swear, I won't make you regret it." I gripped the sheet tighter, my palm sweaty.

As he stroked his beard, I swallowed, my scratchy throat burning for another sip of water as I awaited his judgment.

"I joined the merchant marines when I was eighteen. Fast as I could get out of my house. My pop liked his liquor too. Got nasty when he got deep in the bottle. If I let you stay, you're going to have to work and study. We'll get you GED books, and you'll have to pass, because every real man needs at least a high school education. A strong body isn't shit without a strong mind."

My mouth dropped open. "Thank—"

"Don't thank me yet." He crossed his arms over his wide chest and lifted his chin. "Get healed up and you're on probation. You can't hack it, we send you back, and I'll send a letter stating your condition when we found you and that your uncle was responsible. Maybe they'll put you in foster care instead."

"I can hack it. I promise. You won't regret it."

He nodded. "We'll see about that." He held out a hand and gripped my good one. "I'm Captain Isaac Marcos. This is my ship, the *Fortuna*. Welcome aboard, Jericho Forge."

2

FORGE

Present day

*M*y business is my life. That's one thing that never changes, no matter what. But today, I let myself get sidetracked. *Because of her.*

I never forget meetings. Especially not meetings when one of my business partners has flown halfway across the world to meet on my turf. Today, though, I did. *Because of her.*

India Baptiste—*no*, India Forge—is a distraction I didn't predict, but only because I'm a fucking idiot. I can't even remember the last time I went out of my way to make a woman smile or laugh, let alone change my plans for one. But I did today . . . *because of her.*

Stopping in Saint-Tropez meant screwing up my timeline, and to add insult to injury, *I forgot my meeting with Creighton Karas.*

I toss the keys of my tender to the valet at the pier. "Don't move it. Don't drive it. Don't fucking touch it."

The young blond Brit looks at me slack-jawed as he realizes who I am. "Yes, sir, Mr. Forge. Not a problem, sir. We'll use the other dock for everyone else."

"Good. I'll be back in less than two hours."

He nods again, his brows rising as I peel off a few hundreds from my money clip and hand them over. "Thank you, sir."

As I walk away from the quay, I already want to loosen the tie from around my neck and head back out to sea. For years, I've spent more time on the decks of ships than I have on land, and I like it that way. On the deck of a ship in international waters, the captain's word is law, and he might as well be a god. On land, there are too many variables shifting constantly. *Like wives who smile at you like a hero when you cook her dinner.*

The corner of my mouth tugs upward with a smile, and I wipe it away. *She's too fucking distracting.*

As I approach Nobu, I push the vision away simply for the fact that I liked it too much. When I walk into the new hotel that's certain to be a draw for celebrities on the island wanting to rub elbows with its famous owner, I find the concierge wringing his hands in the lobby and checking his watch.

"Mr. Forge, it's a pleasure. Mr. Karas asked that I bring you right up."

I nod. "Lead the way."

Creighton Karas is one of my newest business partners. Three months ago, I formed a venture with him and Lincoln Riscoff, the heir to America's largest timber company. Our goal was to bring a renewable energy solution to market that would revolutionize the way the shipping world does business. This is one more reason I need Russian steel to build more ships to house the new power production plants that will shock the planet and make all of us very rich men.

We've kept our plans completely silent, because we know

as soon as the fossil-fuel industry gets word, corporate espionage will be out of control.

The concierge leads me through the lobby, with its sun-bleached reclaimed wood paneling and beige and blue tones of the Mediterranean, up the elevator to the penthouse.

"Forge. Good to see you. Thought you'd changed your mind about meeting me," Karas says as he opens the distressed white wooden door on the second knock. The man is a couple of years younger than me, but I've always respected him. I wouldn't have entered into this partnership with him and Riscoff if I hadn't.

I reach out to take the hand he offers. "My apologies. I got caught up."

We shake hands, and then he turns to hold out an arm to a stunning brunette crossing the room. "You remember my wife, Holly?"

"Of course. Mrs. Karas, it's a pleasure."

"Call me Holly. Crey might act all formal, but I don't have time for that nonsense. I was just about to order some appetizers. Would you like anything?"

I think of the fish and lobster I left uneaten. *I'll make it up to India.*

"Thank you, but I'm fine."

She smiles at me and then walks toward her husband. "In that case, I'll head out to the balcony and listen to the artist I'm scouting, and let you two boys talk business." She reaches Karas's side and presses a kiss to his jaw. "Don't take too long."

"I wouldn't dream of it," Karas says, thrusting a hand into her hair to tilt her lips up toward his.

I cut my attention to the blue shimmer of the water beyond the balcony, not wanting to intrude on their private moment.

After Holly leaves the room, Karas walks to the bar and lifts a bottle of Seven Sinners whiskey. "You want one?"

"Absolutely."

As he pours, he cuts right to the heart of the matter at hand. "How are the negotiations progressing with Federov?"

Neither of my business partners have any idea how complex the situation has become, or what I've had to do in order to gain the old Russian's cooperation to even discuss making a deal.

"Complicated."

Karas moves toward me, tumblers in hand and eyebrows raised. "Care to elaborate on that?" he asks as he hands a glass to me.

"He's a cagey old man, and he's proving more difficult to deal with than I expected."

"What do you need from me and Riscoff? We didn't form this partnership to put all the work on your shoulders, Forge. We have plenty of leverage and money. What'll make him cooperate?"

I take a sip of the whiskey and let the warm, peaty taste roll over my tongue. "I have what he wants. I just have to work out a strategy for delivering it in a way that won't compromise anything."

Karas's dark gaze sharpens. "What the hell does the Russian want?"

"His daughter."

His brows shoot higher. "And you have her?"

I turn away from him and walk to the floor-to-ceiling wall of windows where Isla del Cielo is visible in the distance. Sailboats, catamarans, Jet Skis, and speedboats fill the waters between Isaac's island and Ibiza, just like they do every day of the summer.

"I married her."

From behind me, Karas chokes on his drink. "You're

fucking kidding me."

I lift my glass and swallow deeply before shifting to face him. "No. It was a means to an end. The only way I could secure her and the deal."

Karas strides across the room and stops in front of me. "You married her to secure the deal? Jesus fuck, Forge. We're going to have to throw you a bigger cut of the profits for taking one for the team, because I distinctly recall you saying not too many months ago that you'd *never* get married."

How could I forget that? I stood in Karas's California cliffside mansion and swore off marriage right before Riscoff tied the knot.

"I did what needed to be done." I toss down the rest of my drink. "I won't let you or Riscoff down. The ships will be built with Russian steel. The world will be stunned. And we'll all be even richer than you ever planned."

Instead of brightening like I expected, Karas's expression turns thoughtful. "And what about your wife? What does she think about all of this?"

"I don't know. I haven't told her yet. She doesn't even know who the fuck she really is." To myself, I add, *and I have no fucking idea how I'm going to tell her.*

I've never given a shit about collateral damage resulting from doing whatever it takes to close a deal. But for the first time ever, it's all I can think about. *Because of her.*

Karas gives me a worried look. "I hope you know what the hell you're doing, Forge. Because complicated doesn't even begin to cover the situation you're dealing with. Let me get you another drink."

He snags my glass, and I stare out the window toward the island where I left India.

I shouldn't care how this is going to affect her.

But I do, and I have no idea what the fuck I'm going to do about it.

3

INDIA

Bastien's hand wraps around my fingers like a vise, and I know I've made a terrible mistake.

"No, I'm not going anywhere with you." I jerk back, but he won't release me. "Let me go, Bastien!"

"Sorry, Indy. I can't."

He hauls me forward with all his strength, yanking me off my feet. I fly off the dock and over the side of the boat. My head slams into something hard, and pain explodes in my temple.

"No," I mumble as I hear a man yelling my name in the distance.

"Gotta go," Bastien says.

He lowers me to the deck as everything goes black.

4

FORGE

*K*aras runs down the list of action items he and Riscoff have been handling on their end as my phone buzzes incessantly in the pocket of my suit pants. I ignore it for as long as possible, but when it starts up again, my gut says something's wrong.

Karas pauses, and I pull it out.

"Excuse me for a minute." I walk toward the marble fire-place on the opposite end of the living room from the table we'd taken over. "Forge," I snap out in greeting.

"We have a problem, sir." The voice belongs to Donnigan, one of my security people on the island. "Your wife . . ."

An icy shroud settles over me as I prepare for the worst, because somehow, my gut says that's what's coming.

"Where is she?"

"Gone, sir."

I grip the mantel, and the sharp edge of the wood digs into my palm. "How the fuck did she get off the island?"

"By boat. She was down on the dock. I believe it was Bastien de Vere. I don't know if the meeting was prearranged or not. At first it looked voluntary, but then there was a struggle. I'm climbing in the chopper now. We'll pick you up on the roof of the Nobu, sir."

A struggle. The ice melts and my temper boils with rage as I picture de Vere putting his hands on her. *That motherfucker took my wife.*

My jaw clenches, and I grit my teeth. I flex harder on the mantel, needing the bite of pain to keep from punching through the fucking wall.

"Get here. We're going to hunt down that piece of fucking shit. I'm done playing games. I want his fucking head."

I disconnect the call and release the mantel as fury rolls through me. Blood pounds in my head as I face Karas. Normally, I would school my reactions before someone could see my temper, but right now, I don't fucking care.

"What happened?"

"My wife is gone."

"What can I do to help?" he asks, pulling out his phone as he glances out to the balcony where his wife sits in safety. "Between us, we could buy this fucking island. She couldn't have gone far."

I'm already at the door of the suite with my hand on the knob by the time he finishes speaking. "If I need you, I'll let you know."

I miss whatever he says in reply because I'm already headed to the roof.

De Vere is going to die for this.

5

INDIA

*M*y head thumps like it's pressed against a speaker with a relentless beat at a club. Someone flicks water on my face, and I squint one eye open.

"What the hell?" I groan as I roll over on something soft.

"Shit, Indy. I thought your head was harder than that." Bastien's voice grates like nails on a chalkboard.

"What the hell did you do to me?" I reach up to feel for the source of the pain and find a lump beneath my hair, near my temple.

The edge of the mattress depresses as Bastien sits down. "What I had to do—which was get you the fuck away from Forge and his goons."

He touches my hair and I jerk back, not wanting his hands on me. The quick movement sets off another round of explosions in my head.

At my groan, Bastien stands. "Mickey, get her something for her head, and hurry the fuck up."

I blink twice, trying to push through the pain, and open my eyes. The lights are dim and multicolored. I don't recognize the black, white, and red modern decor. The spread beneath me is the color of blood, and I can't help but wonder if mine is on it.

I try to sit up, but the room spins as I rise. Bastien's hands land on my shoulders, as if to steady me, but I slap them away, blinking my eyes open.

"Don't touch me, you piece of shit."

His hands disappear, and through the pounding in my head, I try to remember what the hell happened. Bastien pulled me onto his boat . . . after he told me Forge lied to me about everything. *And I'm not who I think I am.*

The memory slams into my brain, setting off another wave of agony. I dip my head and scrunch the bedcover in my hands as I take long, deep breaths.

"You should've just gotten in the boat, Indy. It didn't have to be this way."

"Fuck you, Bastien." I open my eyes again, if only to glare at his still-blurry form. "Where the hell am I?"

A man in white shorts and a neon-yellow muscle tank, who I assume is Mickey, enters the room. His deeply tanned skin is covered in tattoos. "Here you go, man." He holds out a bottle labeled with a familiar pain reliever logo. "This should do the trick."

Bastien grabs it from him and waits for Mickey to leave before facing me.

"Answer my damn question. Where the hell am I?"

He rolls the bottle between his hands. "You're in a safe place. Forge won't find you here, at least not right away."

I look around the room. There must be a dozen silver suitcases lined up along one wall below a ledge that is covered with liquor bottles. A turntable sits on top of a white desk in the corner, like it's just waiting for a DJ to come in and go to work. Dark shades cover what I assume are large windows, and red LED strip lights lend an eerie glow to the place. Or maybe it's supposed to be a sexy glow. *Ew. Gross.*

"You brought me to your fuck pad? Jesus Christ. Now I need a damn shower." I release my grip on the bedspread.

"Calm down. You're fine."

My wavering vision finally clears and I meet Bastien's gaze, thankful I only see one of him. I haven't seen him since Monte Carlo when his parents cut him off after his sister tattled that I was with him.

"Shouldn't you be back in the UK begging Mummy and Daddy to reinstate your credit cards, and saving your inheritance?"

With a bored expression, Bastien flicks open the lid to the bottle and hands it to me. "I'll get you some water." He walks away without answering a single one of my questions.

Asshole.

Even though I don't want to accept a damn thing from him, when he returns to the side of the bed and offers me water, I snatch it because my head is killing me. I tap three pills into my hand and pop them into my mouth before unscrewing the cap to wash them down.

"Do you remember anything I told you before you hit your head?"

I bare my teeth at him like a feral animal. "You mean when you knocked me unconscious and kidnapped me?"

"You should be thanking me, not looking like you'd rather skin me."

"Not a goddamned chance." I grit out the words. "Now tell me everything, and don't leave out a single fucking thing. Maybe then I won't report you to the cops."

At my threat, Bastien grunts out a laugh. "The police aren't going to help you. As a matter of fact, you need to steer clear of them. They're corrupt as fuck, and probably on Forge's payroll too."

When I growl out his name, Bastien shakes his head and raises his hands as if surrendering, but I know better. He doesn't do anything he doesn't want to do, and he always has an angle. I learned that the hard way.

Before he speaks, he nods at Mickey, who hovers just outside the room. "Close the damn door, but let me know if you spot anyone who shouldn't be here."

Bastien's order reminds me that Forge has to be looking for me. He fucking hates Bastien, and I can't imagine what is going through his head right now.

What if he thinks I went willingly?

I did break my word immediately after Forge and I struck a deal by going straight to the tarmac and hopping on Bastien's jet.

Which is the entire reason I'm in this situation.

The door clicks shut and Bastien paces the room.

"Answer now, or I walk out that door in sixty seconds," I tell him.

Bastien spins around to face me. "You're in that much of a hurry to get back to the man who tricked you into marrying him? The one who's using you and lying to you? I thought you had better instincts than that, Indy. I'm disappointed."

"Sounds like you and Forge have a lot in common then, doesn't it?"

Bastien's expression twists with anger, but it's nothing but a match to my own.

"Spit it out," I say, "or I'm gone."

He walks toward me slowly, pausing an arm's length away. "You won't want to go back to him when I'm done."

"I'm waiting." I push myself to my feet and cross my arms over my chest.

"Your sister's kidnapping was a setup."

The thumping in my head kicks up another notch. "You said that already. Did you do it?"

His head jerks back. "Why the fuck would you ask that?"

"Because how else would you know?"

One side of his mouth lifts in a cruel smirk. "Funny how you question everything I say now, but you didn't bother to question why Forge wanted to marry you."

I know he's changing the subject on purpose, and I'm holding strong. I also know what it feels like to be played by Bastien. When I saw his boat, I should have run the other way.

"You're bluffing. You don't know shit." I take a step toward the door, but Bastien blocks me.

"Am I? Seems you lose your ability to read people when you're not sitting at a poker table."

My hands clench into fists as Bastien turns his back on me and wanders over to the bar. I grit my teeth and take another step toward the door.

"You're not going anywhere, Indy. Not yet." Bastien shoots me a look over his shoulder.

I don't know what his angle is, but he wants something from me. Otherwise, he'd never go to all this trouble. This is no mission of mercy to save me from the big bad wolf.

"I'm pretty sure my *husband* is going to have something to say when he finds out you *kidnapped me*."

Bastien spins around to spear me with his icy glare before replacing the liquor bottle and stalking toward me. "You think Forge is the fucking hero here, and I'm the villain? Fuck no. You've got it dead wrong. He's the one who tricked you into marrying him, remember?"

I take another step toward the door. "Isn't that what you were going to do if I said yes? Or did you forget that little proposal you made already?"

"I didn't forget shit." Bastien's nostrils flare. "But I also wouldn't have used your sister as leverage. That's what he did, right? Because he had her the *whole fucking time*."

The lobster and fish I ate earlier threaten to make a reappearance on the white tile floor.

"You're lying," I say, my tone ragged as my stomach twists. *I don't want to believe it. I can't believe it. Who would be so horrible?*

"You don't have to believe me," Bastien says with a smirk. "You can figure that shit out for yourself. All you gotta do is *think*, Indy."

I dig my nails into my palms as I try to steady myself. I know what Bastien's trying to do—make me question everything. *And it's working.*

I flip through the memories of how Forge said he'd help me get my sister back, but only if I said yes to his no-questions-asked favor that would be *financially beneficial* to him.

I remember the shock I felt when the chopper touched down on the deck of the yacht and Summer stumbled out. I couldn't believe she was already there and safe. I was too stupid and happy and grateful to ask the million questions that popped into my mind about how he managed it.

Forge didn't kidnap her. There's no way. *Is there?*

When I don't reply, Bastien continues.

"Actions speak louder than words, right? You know none of this adds up. He's been playing you since day one. Fuck, even before day one. You think he walked into that card game at La Reina by accident?" Bastien taps his chin. "I wonder who told him about it? Jean Phillippe, maybe?"

I swallow. "Give me one good reason why Forge would do any of this."

Bastien's lips twist into a predatory smile. "No one gets something for nothing around here."

Of course. Of course he wants something from me. I can only imagine what it is.

"Not so quick to ask questions now, are you?" His smug tone makes me want to backhand the smirk off his face.

Play the man, not the game. Pull it together, Indy. He's trying to bait you.

"That's not it," I tell him, my tone frigid this time. "I just know you won't answer a single one. I shouldn't be surprised either. You always go back on your word."

Bastien's expression sharpens. "What the fuck does that mean?"

"You said you'd tell me everything if I came with you. My instincts to run the other way were absolutely right."

"And stay with Forge? He's the one who fucked you over . . ." His lip curls as he drags his gaze up and down my body. "Literally and figuratively."

A greasy feeling pools in my stomach and I sidestep toward the door. "You want me to believe he's the bad guy in this scenario? Give me proof."

Bastien laughs caustically. "I didn't peg you to be so fucking naive, Indy. Answer one question for me—did he make you sign a prenup?"

I freeze. It's the same question I asked myself. *How the hell could Bastien know to ask that?*

"If only your face was this expressive at the poker table. You'd never fucking win," Bastien says with a cruel grin. His index finger taps the rim of the glass. "So, no prenup . . . Did you even bother to ask yourself why a billionaire would commit financial suicide by getting married without a prenup?"

I may as well have turned into a statue, because I did ask myself the question . . . and just let it go like a freaking idiot.

Bastien's tapping stops as his grin turns shark-like. "One answer . . . because he has more to gain than to lose by marrying you."

"I'm broke, Bastien. What the hell could Forge possibly have to gain?"

A fractured memory comes back as Bastien crosses the room to sit on the bed.

"Forge is using you to get what he wants from your father."

But I don't have a father.

Bastien pats the mattress beside him. "Why don't you sit down, Indy. It's a long story."

6

FORGE

*D*eath by a thousand cuts was the wrong way to play Isaac's revenge. I should have killed de Vere. If he were dead, I wouldn't be in this situation.

Now I'm going to kill him with my bare hands, and I don't give a fuck who he is.

His father can scream down the House of Lords, and it will make absolutely no difference to me. *De Vere took my wife.* Somehow, he's involved in this whole fucking mess, and I don't know how. *Yet.*

"You're sure she was drunk? Not unconscious?" I demand answers from the blond twenty-something kid who works the marina where Bastien's sleek red Donzi is docked.

"I don't know. People are always carrying other people off boats after they've had too much. It's not my job to ask questions."

I curl my hands into fists and fight the urge to pick this guy up and toss him off the dock, because it's not going to do me any good.

"He didn't say where he was going?" Donnigan asks.

"No. He just put her in the car and left. I didn't see which way he went. We had another boat coming in—"

Useless fuck. I turn away and head back to the chopper where a crowd has gathered around it on the quay.

"Let's go. This is a waste of time."

Donnigan matches my stride by the time we reach the helicopter. "Where to next?"

"His villa. He just might be stupid enough to go there."

Once we climb in the chopper and put on the headsets, Donnigan radios the tower again, but they refuse to clear our takeoff after our unsanctioned landing. Donnigan looks to me.

I reach out and flip the channel on the radio so the tower can't hear us. "Go. I'll pay their fines. Just avoid the goddamned planes."

With a nod, he takes off, and within minutes, we reach a large white house situated in the hills. It's Bastien's party pad, although not for much longer, if his parents really cut him off.

A red Lamborghini winds its way down the curved driveway.

"Set it down right in front of him. Don't let that fucker get away."

Donnigan doesn't question my orders. The car speeds up as we approach, and I motion to the ground.

"Now!"

The driver slams on the brakes as the helicopter touches down on the pavement. I whip my harness off and jump out.

"What the hell," the driver yells from the window, but he goes quiet when he sees me charging at him. His hands flutter in the car, and the window slides up.

I yank open the door before he can lock it. "Where the fuck is de Vere? He inside?"

The driver, a dark-haired Spaniard with a thick gold chain

hanging around his neck and a goatee throws his hands in the air. "I don't know shit, man. I made a wrong turn. Bad address."

"Lying sack of shit. You're going to fucking tell me where de Vere is right now." I grab the chain and twist it around my hand.

"I'm just the help. I don't know anything. I swear."

My gaze narrows on his fear-filled eyes as his hands claw at the chain tightening around his neck.

"The help drives a Lambo? Not a fucking chance. I'm going to ask you one more time, and if you don't tell me what I want to know, I'll take you up in that chopper and drop you in the middle of the fucking ocean. You understand? Where the fuck is de Vere?"

"No! I don't—"

His words choke off when I tug the chain to pull him out of the car. Donnigan throws open the back door as we approach the chopper, and the guy flails harder with every step I take.

"Please, man. Don't kill me. He's not home."

I shove him toward the open door and look to Donnigan. "Go check the house. If he's lying, he dies."

The guy crosses himself. "He's not there. I swear. He had me pick up some shit, and I'm supposed to meet him at a friend's place."

"Tell. Me. Where." I grit out the words through clenched teeth.

THE ROTOR WASH kicks up dust as we land on another roof that was never meant to be used as a helipad. Thanks to the punk in the Lambo, we know one of de Vere's friends leases the entire top floor of this building for parties and as a stash house for the drugs de Vere traffics on his clueless parents' private jet.

He's going down, and there won't be anyone to save him.

Donnigan stays in the chopper as I hop out and head for the door marked STAIRS. It swings open as I approach, and Goliath's familiar form waves me on. As I jog down the flights behind him, I send up a vow to Isaac.

You'll be able to rest easy soon, my friend. I'm going to end it.

Goliath shoulders open the door that leads to the penthouse level, and I step out behind him, gun in hand. The hallway is empty, but I spot the door closest to the sea side of the building, which is where the rat in the chopper said we'd find de Vere.

I nod at it, and Goliath approaches it at my side. We stand in front of the door and he motions like he's going to handle it, but I hold up a finger as Donnigan's words roll through my head again.

"At first it looked voluntary, but then there was a struggle."

Banked rage roars to the surface, and I take a step back before ramming the sole of my shoe into the door beside the handle with every bit of force my six-foot-three, two-hundred-thirty-pound frame can muster.

The door swings wide and whacks into the opposite wall.

With guns drawn, Goliath and I rush inside toward a man jolting up from where he was bent over a table, a rolled bill held nearly to his nose.

"What the fuck! You can't—" His protest cuts off when his gaze lands on the Glock in my hand and the giant at my side. "What do you want? I don't have any cash."

Another door swings open, and de Vere leans against the frame.

"He doesn't want your cash, Mickey. He came for something very, very different." De Vere looks over his shoulder. "Isn't that right, Indy?"

7

INDIA

*H*e's here. Forge is here.

I push out of the chair where I parked myself behind the desk with the turntable to keep my distance from Bastien while he proceeded to toss back drink after drink and talk shit about Forge.

As soon as I'm on my feet, the room wobbles from side to side. *From hitting my head?* I hold on to the desk for support and take another step toward Forge's voice. Everything feels weird, including the smooth, cool wood beneath my fingertips.

I blink a few times, trying to get the room to stop spinning, but it doesn't help. My palms are clammy and sweat breaks out on my brow. *Something's wrong.*

I look around the room, and the light hurts my eyes.

I'm fucked up. What the hell is going on? I attempt another step toward the door, but cool air hits my skin and tremors ripple over me.

I have to sit down. I stumble toward the bed and plop onto it, gripping the red coverlet with my fists to stay upright.

"Sorry, Forge. Your *wife* is in no hurry to leave my bed." Bastien's lazy drawl reeks of innuendo.

"Get the fuck out of my way, de Vere." Forge's voice deepens to the point where it's almost inaudible.

My head bobs as I try to stand again. *Nope.* I shut my eyes, hoping that will help me regain a modicum of balance or control.

"Feel free to stay in bed, Indy. You don't have to leave with him if you don't want to." Bastien's tone is even more smug now, and I don't need to see him to know that he must be grinning like the cat who got the cream.

What the hell is happening to me? I shouldn't feel like—

Then I remember the pills I took out of the pain reliever bottle.

He drugged me. Bastien fucking drugged me. *Again.*

8

FORGE

*W*ith the gun pressed to de Vere's chest, I lower my voice. "Move, or I won't hesitate to pull this fucking trigger."

De Vere shows no fear, which shocks me because he's always been a fucking pussy. "You won't do it. You would've killed me years ago if you had the balls, but you don't."

Despite his bold words, he backs into the room and moves to the side, revealing India sitting on the bed, slowly rocking back and forth like she's catatonic.

"What the hell did you do to her?" I demand.

"I told her some of the truth." He laughs, but clearly he's the only person who thinks there's a damn thing funny about this situation. "Isn't that right, my dear? Why don't you tell Forge how upset you were when you found out he lied about your sister's rescue to get you to marry him?"

"Why should I believe either of you?"

When India finally looks directly at me, I realize something's very wrong. Her blue eyes are nearly solid black from her completely blown pupils.

"What the fuck did you give her?" I jab the gun into de Vere's chest where his shirt hangs open.

"Whoa . . ." India stands with her arms out to the side for balance, and sways back and forth like she's on the deck of a ship sailing through a gale. She blinks a few times before rubbing her hands down her face. "I'm fucked up."

"Goliath. Cover de Vere." I hear a grunt from out in the living room, and I hope it means Mickey has been restrained.

Goliath trains his gun on de Vere, and I reach out for India.

"Come here. I got you." I hold out my left hand, but she zeroes in on the pistol in my right.

"I don't like guns." Her words come out slurred.

De Vere snorts a laugh and then grunts, telling me Goliath probably shut him up.

As soon as the gun is out of sight, Indy takes another step and I catch her in my arms. I do a quick rundown before pulling her into my side to support her unsteady legs.

Flushed. Body temp higher than normal. Pupils blown. She's rolling.

I look to de Vere. "Molly? Ecstasy? Some other party drug you cooked up?"

"Nothing she hasn't had before, I'm sure," de Vere says, his tone mocking.

India's arm slides around my back, and her face presses against my jacket. "This is soft. Really soft." She rubs her cheek along the Italian linen like a kitten with a silky blanket.

"She'll be fine in a few hours," de Vere says, and my gaze snaps to his. "At least, until she starts asking you who her father is and why you'd marry her without a prenup. When you tell her that she's the daughter of—"

"I don't have a father," Indy says as she buries her face in my jacket. "I never have. Never will. And I don't want to hear another goddamned thing about it. Fuck him. Fuck you. Fuck everyone."

Goliath presses the barrel of his gun to de Vere's temple.

"You heard her. She doesn't want to hear a fucking thing you have to say."

De Vere's leer fades to a grimace. "She'll find out the truth eventually. Even if you have your henchman end me right now. Which you won't. Because you can't even give the order to pull the fucking trigger."

Blood pounds in my temple, and my jaw clenches. More than anything, I want to pull the gun from where I shoved it and squeeze the trigger until every round is buried in de Vere's body. But he's right about one thing—I won't give Goliath the order to do it. De Vere's death belongs to me. For Isaac. For his vengeance. For my own fucking peace.

"I don't like guns." India tugs away from my body, and de Vere's smug laughter echoes off the walls of the room.

Against every single instinct I have, I nod to Goliath to lower his gun. It's not like he can't keep de Vere in line just as easily without one.

I pull Indy tighter against me, but she continues to struggle. "It's gone. No more guns." Only when I say the words does she stop fighting me.

De Vere's frozen stare rakes over where I hold her in my arms. "You might have her now, but you'll never be able to keep her." He pauses to straighten his shirt. "But then again, that was never the plan, was it, Forge? You're going to get what you need from Indy's rich daddy and pay her off well enough that you never have to see her again. I bet you have it all planned out."

"Shut your fucking mouth."

"Or what? You're going to shoot me? You're not man enough. Just like you're not man enough to tell her the truth. But don't worry. She'll find out soon enough."

De Vere's lips stretch into a mocking smile.

"Indy wouldn't listen today, but when she learns for herself, she's going to walk away and fuck up every one of your plans. I can't wait to watch her leave you and take your money with her. Should've had her sign a prenup . . . but we both know why you didn't."

INDIA

Prenup. Prenup. Prenup.

The word beats in my head, and I know I should ask why I didn't sign one, but I'm too entertained by rubbing my face against Forge's suit.

Lights and colors swirl in my brain as I let my eyes close again. "It's bright."

As soon as I speak, Forge stiffens. "Keep your eyes closed. We're leaving right now. I'm picking you up."

I do as he says, enjoying the light show in my mind much more than the harsh glare of sunlight coming from the other room, but my head spins as he lifts me off the floor.

"Whoa. Whoa." I wrap my arms around his neck for stability.

"I can't believe you'd even consider going with him. What a fucking joke," Bastien says, sounding like a spoiled little boy who lost a game he thought was fixed. "I didn't lie to you, Indy. That's all he'll do. He'll never tell you a fucking bit of the truth. You're his pawn, not his wife."

Forge's arms tighten around me. "Don't you fucking speak to her."

Forge barks out the command, and even though I know I should be asking for answers to all the questions Bastien raised, I don't care right now.

I want to be angry, but I can't summon the emotion when I'm pressed against the silky material of Forge's suit, breathing in the sandalwood and fresh man scent. His fingertips brush my arm over and over, soothing me, and I soak up the sensation. I wish he could trail his fingertips all over me and not just that small patch of skin.

It's the drugs. I've taken party drugs before, so I know what's happening, and I also know there's nothing I can do but ride it out and maybe even enjoy it.

Stupid, Indy.

The critical voice in my head tells me I'm an idiot, and it's probably right. But my brain just dumped every bit of my serotonin, dopamine, and norepinephrine into my system, and every sensation feels amazing. It's been years since I've felt this incredible.

I nuzzle his neck, wanting to get another hint of the scent coming off his skin. One of my hands reaches up to comb through the too-long ends of his black hair. *Ooh, smooth and silky.* I curl the locks around my fingers, and he lets me.

He's so warm and strong and cuddly. At least, right now he is. No doubt, as soon as the drug wears off in a few hours, my entire world will come crashing to a halt, and Forge will once again be a prickly beast. Maybe it makes me a coward or a moron, but I'd rather enjoy this hazy, happy feeling rather than hurry up the inevitable return of cold reality.

I also don't want to be anywhere near Bastien when I come down, because I'll want to kill him. The next wave of sensation hits me, and my head and fingers drop against Forge's shoulder.

"I need to lay down."

His breath caresses my cheek as he replies. "We're

leaving now." His lips brush the shell of my ear as his head lifts and he speaks to Bastien.

"Goliath will make sure you don't follow us. Your friend who was driving the red Lambo will be on the roof if you're looking for him."

1 0

FORGE

J've never carried cargo so precious or been so fucking worried about another person as I make my way into the villa and head straight for my bedroom. Every minute of the short flight to Isla del Cielo, I kept Indy close to me, brushing my hand over her forehead to check her temperature in between giving her sips of water.

Over the years, I've seen plenty of people in her state, and not once has a single one of them had any adverse complications. However, just to be certain, and because of the knot on her head, Donnigan contacted my private physician. He told us to watch her, try not to cause her any distress, and he could be out within thirty minutes if we needed him.

Indy's not showing any signs to cause concern, but I'm not about to take chances or spend a minute not watching her like I have her under a microscope.

"Are you too warm?" I ask her as I lay her on the bed and press the button on the remote to automatically close all the shades to shield her eyes.

"A little," Indy replies as she rolls over onto her back and snags the hem of her shirt to pull it up over her head. Thankfully, she's still wearing the bikini she bought in Saint-Tropez beneath it. Then she wriggles out of her skirt, and I untangle it from between her feet.

"Better?"

"I want a shower. That would feel so good."

Her eyes are closed and her tone is languid. Because I have every interest in keeping her body temperature within safe ranges, I agree with her suggestion.

"You can open your eyes now. It's dark enough. I'll get the shower running."

I rise to step away, but she reaches out and grasps my wrist. I look down into her big black pupils and faintly see the slivers of blue around them.

"I'm okay, Forge." Her features take on a serious cast. "You don't have to take care of me. I'm not going to die and screw up your plans. Don't be nice to me if you're just trying to cover your own ass. I don't trust you either."

Her honesty, whether a side effect of the drug or not, is like an elbow to the gut, and I wish I didn't deserve the disdain her words convey.

"India, I have things I have to tell you," I say, but she shakes her head.

"Don't fuck up my roll, Forge. It might not have been my choice, but I'm going to enjoy this before I have to face reality."

INDIA

orge's lips press together, and he nods before walking toward the wide doorway that must lead to the en-suite bathroom. As soon as I hear water, a rush of power sweeps over me.

I gave Forge an order, and he followed it.

The entire way home, he watched me like a hawk, lines forming in the tanned skin around his eyes.

Either Forge feels something for me whether he wants to or not . . . or Bastien's right, and Forge is just protecting his asset because he needs me. I don't know which it is, but I don't want to be any man's pawn.

All I've ever wanted is a life that couldn't be ripped away from me at any given moment. Safety. Stability. The knowledge that I would fall asleep every night with my head on the pillow I chose to sleep on, not somewhere I was forced to be out of necessity and survival.

Do I truly have a father? Is that why Forge married me? Did he really kidnap my sister just so he could manipulate me?

That's a plan I could see Bastien hatching, but not so much Forge, unless I'm wildly wrong about him.

Or because I've been dick-struck and I want at least one more ride on the Kraken before I tell him I never want to see him again.

Forge steps out of the bathroom, holding a fluffy white robe. "The shower's ready when you are."

I shove all the thoughts out of my head and latch onto the only thing that matters right now. *This gorgeous billionaire of a man is here to do my bidding.*

I don't know why that knowledge gives me such a thrill, but it does, and I'm going to embrace it for as long as I can. Maybe it's the same reason I love to win at poker against rich and powerful men who don't think I have the skill or the nerve to bluff them out of their fortunes.

Yep, I've probably got daddy issues.

The next wave of the drug hits me as I swing my feet over the side of the bed. When I rise on wobbly legs, Forge strides forward.

"I'll carry you."

I hold out a hand, and when he freezes in place, I have to hide my grin. *He really does what I command.* It takes all my concentration not to let out a giggle.

"I can walk." I pause. "But I'll take your arm. For balance, I mean."

With his thickly stubbled jaw tensing, he nods, and I can't help but wonder how much doing my bidding costs him.

Seems fair to me.

I grip his arm with my right hand. The extra sway in my hips means that I bump him with every step, and I won't even apologize for it. When we reach the bathroom, the lights have been dimmed to almost pure darkness, which my eyes certainly appreciate. There's even a candle on the rough-edged rock countertop that makes me smile.

He's actually trying to make this better for me.

When I stop in front of the carwash-sized glass shower enclosure, I know exactly what I'm going to do next.

Forge reaches for the handle and opens the door, releasing the barest hint of steam. I'm impressed he knew not to turn the water too hot because he doesn't want me to have hyperthermia and organ failure, which is the biggest risk of club drugs like whatever Bastien's asshole friend gave me.

Before I can chastise myself for being so naive as to take *any* kind of pill they gave me, I remind myself that at least my head doesn't hurt at all, and I get to put off reality for at least another six hours. Which means going back to my initial idea—

Enjoy the shit out of this. Because once I wake up, I'm gone, and whatever plans Forge had are over.

I reach for the tie on my bathing suit top, and Forge touches my arm to still my movement.

"Keep it on." His voice sounds strangled, and not at all like the man who has been playing with my libido for the last few days.

I shoot him a sideways glance as I tug the tie free. "If I don't care about you catching the full show, why would you?"

"Goddammit—"

"Shut up, Forge."

I drop the tie and my breasts spill free of the top. But because he's a contrary man, Forge doesn't look down. He keeps staring directly into my eyes.

Try to ignore me, I say silently. *I dare you.*

I reach around the back and tug the knot to release it completely before I shove the bottoms over my hips. The healing cut on my side twinges, but not enough to dull the decadent feeling of the cool air wafting over my skin. My nipples peak, and I can't wait to get under the warm water.

Stepping around Forge, who still hasn't looked anywhere but my face, I walk into the shower and moan as the spray touches my skin.

"God, that feels so good." I groan as I tip my head back and let the water beat down over my hair. Reveling in the sensation, I sway from side to side.

"Jesus Christ. Sit down. I'm not taking another chance that you're going to fall and crack your head."

A smile stretches my lips wide. "If you're going to give me orders while I'm naked, you better make them dirtier than that." I open my eyes to see Forge's jaw tick and his Adam's apple bob in his throat.

"Indy . . ."

"Only my friends call me Indy, and you're not one of them."

1 2

FORGE

*H*er statement slices me again, even though I shouldn't care what she thinks of me.

She's a means to an end, I remind myself, but I know I'm lying. She *was* a means to an end. Sometime in the last forty-eight hours, that changed. Now she has become something much more dangerous and unpredictable.

Indy presses her fingertips to her forehead before dragging them down her body, and it's impossible not to follow them as she skims over her face, her chin, her chest, and then her tits, where she pauses to circle a tightly budded nipple. My teeth grate together at the thought of pulling it into my mouth and teasing it with my tongue before sucking hard and giving it a sharp tug.

She's taunting me in the most daring way possible.

"I know you want me," Indy says, her words coming out on a purr as she destroys more of my self-control. "And right now, maybe for the last time ever, I want you too."

Fuck. Fuck. Fuck.

I can't touch her. Not now. Not like this.

But she's right, this might be the last chance I ever have.

Maybe that's my punishment for doing what I've done. Getting one shot at the thing I didn't know I'd want most, and then having it ripped away from me forever.

Still, it wouldn't be right. I might have gotten to where I am by being an opportunistic asshole, but something about taking advantage of her in this state doesn't feel right . . . no matter how much I don't want to care about morals or ethics at this moment.

I shake my head. "You can't handle me, little girl."

Her eyes roll as she tilts her head from side to side, arching her spine. Her fingers continue lower, skimming over her curved stomach and then to the shaved section right above her pussy.

"Bullshit. You're the one who can't handle me. I know exactly what I'm asking for. I want you to touch me and fuck me and make me come until I can forget every goddamned thing while I ride this out." Her eyes snap open and she stares me down. "But you can tell yourself you're being a martyr by not taking advantage. I'll touch myself. Fuck myself. And pretend it's you instead."

Well, fuck.

As soon as her fingertips slide over her clit, my self-control jumps its chain, demanding I strip and follow her into the water for one last taste of the promised land. Indy moans my name as she thrusts her finger between her pink folds, and the battle is over before it even started.

I rip off my tie, kick off my shoes, strip out of my jacket, shirt, and pants, and follow her in—just in time for her to spin around on her toes and lose her balance. My heart in my throat, I lurch forward with my arms outstretched, and catch her slippery, naked body against mine as the water streams down over us both.

Indy's lashes, darkened from the water, flutter as she

looks up at me. "You caught me. I guess that means you get to keep me—for tonight."

Her blue eyes are still largely black, but there's something in her gaze that brings out every protective instinct I've ever had. I want to shield her from the harsh reality of the world outside these walls, from me, from Bastien, from her father, from herself.

I want to slay fucking dragons for this woman—even though I'm one of them.

But right now, with the slick skin of her naked body sliding against mine and the puckered beads of her nipples pressing against my chest, I push it all aside. She's right . . . tomorrow will be here soon enough, and in the sober light of morning, this sweet and naked Indy will be gone for good.

What kind of man would I be if I pushed away what might be my last chance at paradise?

A stupid one. And no one has accused me of being stupid in a long time.

I slide my hands down her body to cup the cheeks of her ass and pull her against me.

"You're so hard," she whispers, her eyes closed again as she tips her head back and the water sheets off her thick mane of hair. Her fingers wrap around my biceps and squeeze, as if testing their strength. "And so strong. Strong enough to tear me apart with your bare hands."

It's on the tip of my tongue to promise that I'll never hurt her, but that would be a lie. The omissions I've already made will shred any trust she could ever place in me, destroy any feelings for me I can't help but wish she had.

"I'll protect you with them instead," I tell her, lifting her. "Wrap your legs around my waist. I want to hold you."

I don't know where the order comes from, because I've never told a woman I want to hold her before. Actually, I've never *wanted* to hold a woman like this before.

Indy complies, and her calves cross over my ass, putting her pussy directly against my dick. It's fucking torture of the most perfect kind.

More than anything, I want to pick her up and slide her down on my cock, but this isn't about what I want. This is about giving her what she needs. Maybe in some hidden recess of my mind, I'm hoping that if I make tonight good enough for her, she won't demand a divorce and walk right out the door tomorrow.

Unlikely.

But still, the optimist in me decides it's worth a shot.

"Hold me under the water. It feels so good."

"Whatever you want, baby," I say, letting the endearment slip out.

Indy's eyes snap open and she shakes her head. "Don't use that throwaway shit on me. Ever." She rocks her hips, rubbing her clit against my dick, and it feels like the most incredible punishment she could ever devise.

"I can't call you Indy because we're not friends."

"True." With her eyes drifting closed again, Indy drops her head back and allows it to loll back and forth, dragging her hair through the spray of the showerhead. "I guess your options are wife, prize, the pawn, ace in the hole . . . Does it really matter? Pretty soon, I won't be anything to you."

She cuts to the heart of the matter so effectively that I have to wonder what the hell de Vere told her. Then again, de Vere shouldn't have *any* information to give her . . . unless he's involved with the Russians. Which means Federov's playing me—or he has a leak in his organization.

But that can all wait until I don't have my naked wife in my arms who forbade me from fucking up her roll.

"Ace in the hole. I like that one," I tell her absently as I lift her higher so I can finally pull one nipple into my mouth and suck.

"Oh God, that feels so good." Indy rocks, rubbing her slick pussy and that little silver piercing against my abs as my dick presses snug against her ass crack. *Where she's a virgin.*

Never in my life have I been so turned on by the idea of being the one to take a woman's virginity—any kind of virginity. But with Indy . . . things are different.

As soon as this is over, she'll be determined to forget me and everything that happened between us, and I have a feeling I'll be doing the opposite. I'll hold on to every memory, jacking myself into oblivion as I try to forget this woman.

"You're going to come just by rubbing that tight little cunt against me while I do this." I bite down on the nipple closest to my mouth and scrape it with my teeth.

"Oh . . ." Indy moans, rocking harder, like she's already chasing an orgasm. "More."

I switch nipples, scraping, biting, tugging, and sucking on the other one until her whimpers fill the shower stall and the slickness on my abs has nothing to do with the water pouring from the fixtures in the shower.

"I can't—" She bucks against me. "I need more."

"I'll give you what you need," I tell her, sliding my hand around one ass cheek to press the pad of my index finger against her asshole.

"Oh God. Oh God. Yes."

I slide my fingers up further to sweep back the wetness soaking her pussy and use it to lube up the clenched muscle trying to keep me out.

"I'm going to finger-fuck your tight little asshole. Don't try to keep me out."

"Please!"

Another surge of blood rushes to my dick at her cry. I push through the resistance, and her ass opens for me like a damn miracle.

Indy's pleas turn to screams as her whole body convulses with pleasure. Her asshole tightens around my finger, signaling wave after wave of her orgasm. When her body finally goes limp and her legs fall from around my waist, I pull my finger free and lower her until her feet touch the tile floor.

"No. Don't put me down. I can't—"

She doesn't have to say it twice. I sweep her up into my arms, holding her like a treasured bride I'm about to carry over the threshold.

But I didn't do that, because I was never supposed to feel anything about her other than the satisfaction I'd get from achieving my goals.

With her cheek resting against my chest, I wonder if it's even possible to undo how badly I've fucked up this situation.

"Time for bed."

She nods, and I move us out of the spray, shouldering open the door.

"It's cold," Indy protests, and I grab the robe she wouldn't take before.

In the dim light of the bathroom, her features look lazy and relaxed as I settle her on her feet, wrap the robe around her, and tuck her arms into the sleeves before tying the belt.

"You need water."

She tries to step out of my hold, but I lift her again, loving the weight of her in my arms because she's real and solid and *mine*. Even if it's only for tonight. Part of me wants to thank de Vere for his fuckup, because it's a gift that I won't squander.

I lay her on the massive bed and pull the coverlet up over her exposed toes before grabbing a bottle of water and removing the cap. As she sips, I realize her hair is soaking through her pillow.

"Don't move. I'll be right back."

I head for the bathroom and grab a thick towel, and also the candle I lit for God only knows what misguided reason. But I saw the way she looked at it, and I liked it.

With the flickering flame safely on the nightstand, I wrap the towel around her hair and squeeze out as much of the water as I can.

"It's going to be a mess in the morning," Indy mumbles.

"Quit worrying."

Her eyes open and she looks at me. "We already know how this is going to end. You stonewalling and refusing to tell me anything. Then I'll get pissed and walk away." Her tone sounds so matter-of-fact, like there's no other possible option.

Bullshit. I'll find another option.

"You don't know that," I tell Indy as her eyes drift closed again.

"Yes, I do. Because you won't ever bend or change. You don't know how, Forge. You always get your way, even if it means bulldozing anything standing in your path." She shifts to lay her cheek on the pillow. "But I don't much like being flattened. So that means I have to get out of your way before you crush me." A tear leaks from one eye and trickles down the smooth, tanned skin of her face.

Knowing what I know about MDMA, the words she's speaking are what she believes are the absolute truth. And maybe she's right. I am a bulldozer. I don't let anything or anyone stop me from achieving my goals. I've never considered the human cost before, but Indy's sad statement makes me picture it much too vividly.

Is closing this deal worth destroying her?

Before I can answer that question, Indy tugs at the tie of the robe and kicks at the blankets.

"I'm hot, and I want you to eat my pussy."

13

INDIA

When I'm rolling, I have no control over my words. They spill out of my lips freely, just like the tears I swipe away from my eyes.

I shouldn't care that Forge's ambition will flatten me if I don't run like hell in the other direction, but obviously I care too much.

Don't think about it right now.

So instead of thinking, I flip open the sides of my robe and spread my legs like there's not a single trace of shame or modesty in my entire body. And right now, there isn't. I want him to make me come again like he did in the shower.

When his finger pressed into my ass, I came unglued. The pleasure from it threatened to send me falling right to the floor, which is what I would have done if his strong arms and broad shoulders hadn't been there to hold me up.

What would it be like to always know someone would be there to catch you, no matter what? That you will never fall? That you're safe?

Another tear tracks down my face because I know that I'll never be able to answer those questions.

"Why the tears, Ace?" Forge catches one on his thumb, and I brush his hand away.

When I threw out that nickname, I was completely joking. But for some reason, I like the way it sounds rolling off his tongue in that gruff voice.

"I don't know what you're talking about," I say, but he grips my wrists in one hand and pulls them down to my lap. One by one, Forge wipes the tears from my cheeks, but instead of stopping, they come faster.

"You're killing me here."

I squeeze my eyes shut and try to make them stop, but I know it won't work.

"Make me scream instead," I blurt.

His touch falls away from my face, and the bed shifts as he moves lower. Forge's palms skim down my thighs and send goose bumps rising across my skin.

"I can do that. Just lay back and enjoy."

As soon as his hot breath washes over my center, I open my eyes and stare down at the dark head of hair between my legs. It falls forward, obscuring my view, but it doesn't matter. I can feel what he's doing to me just fine. When his tongue sweeps from the bottom of my pussy, all the way up— almost to my clit—I thread my fingers through his hair and grip.

"Don't tease me."

He lifts his face to meet my gaze. "That, I can't promise." His wide tongue lashes out and flicks my clit. "But you'll be screaming my name when you come."

We both know he's right, and he sets out to prove it to me in undisputable fashion. His tongue darts inside me, and he groans.

"So fucking delicious. I could eat you all night."

"Mmm." I moan in approval because I wouldn't object . . . at least, not until I was dying for him to fill me.

Somehow, he must be able to read my mind, because with his left hand, he presses a thick finger against my opening and it slides inside. I buck against his mouth as he sucks my clit hard. It doesn't take long before my first orgasm is barreling down on me, and I'm on the edge.

With a forceful plunge, his finger fills me, and I scream as I let go.

"I can't—"

"Not stopping yet. You haven't screamed my name. I want to hear it."

14

FORGE

I don't know why I care so much, but I'm a man on a mission. I want to hear Indy say it. Not Forge —*Jericho*. And I'm going to make her come over and over again until she breaks down and gives me what I want.

Is it fair? I don't fucking care. I've never cared about fair before, and I won't start now when I'm going to lose her tomorrow.

I lube up my thumb and go back to work, fucking her pussy with my finger as I slide my thumb into her ass while I suck and bite her clit.

Indy's head swings back and forth on the pillow, and when mixed with the effects of the drug, the pleasure has to be more overwhelming than what she's experienced lately. *Actually . . .* I remember what she said earlier. *I'm the only man who has touched her in ten years.*

Whatever happens next, I'm going to make one thing certain—the memory of me and what happens tonight will be burned in her brain in a way that she'll never forget it.

"Forge! I can't—"

I pull out my thumb and slide it back in. "Say my name,

dammit."

Her cry breaks as her ass tenses. She's coming again, and that's when she gives me what I want, even if it's only a whisper to start.

"*Jericho.*"

I bite down hard on her clit, and her entire body shakes as my name grows louder into a scream. I lift my head, but her hands bury in my hair and keep my face planted between her legs.

"More."

It's another plea, and one I can't ignore. I also know that it's selfish as fuck, but if I'm going to give her another orgasm, it's going to happen with my dick buried so deep inside her tight little cunt that I'll never forget the feel of her. I want the memory of her burned into me too.

I pull away, not caring that strands of my hair stay gripped within her fingers. I fumble for the drawer of the nightstand, minding the candle on the top, and roll a condom down my dick. As soon as I'm covered, I move between her legs and plow forward.

Her inner walls flutter and clamp down as tears stream from Indy's closed eyes. I want to see them, even with the darkness almost completely shadowing the light.

"Look at me."

Her eyes open, and with our gazes locked, I pound into her over and over, fucking her as if everything depends on this being the best goddamned night of her life.

And maybe it does.

This is the one thing I can give her without holding anything back. All of me for all of her.

Her lids flutter, like she wants to close them, but I find her clit and press down. *Detonation.*

"Yes! Jericho! Yes!"

My orgasm pours out of me as soon as she says my name.

INDIA

*a*s sleep fades away, my body feels heavy, like it's weighed down by a truckload of cement. I try to lift my arm, but it's pinned beneath an immovable object.

I open my eyes, but the room is pitch black. The only sound is the quiet breathing of the man beside me. The one whose entire body is wrapped around mine.

Forge. Or Jericho, as I called him last night as he wrenched more pleasure from my body than I've ever experienced.

As much as I want to say it was all the drugs, I know it's a lie. Sure, they might heighten the experience, but nothing can make a bad lover into an incredible one.

Forge is more than incredible, and that can't just be my limited scale of experience doing the measuring. He strikes me as a man ruthless in every aspect—especially when it comes to pleasing his partner in bed.

And you've got to stop being all dick-struck, Indy. It's morning, and the reality check hits me hard, even as my tongue sticks to the roof of my mouth.

I tug my arm out from under Forge and roll over to see a bottle of water on the nightstand. *Thank you, Lord.* But I know it's not the Lord I need to be thanking.

With quiet and careful movements, I roll out of bed, hoping like hell I don't wake the sleeping beast. I need a shower, food, and to get my feet firmly under me before I'm ready for the confrontation that's coming.

I take the water bottle into the shower and try not to think about how I lost every single hint of inhibition last night and taunted him into joining me. Hot shame flushes my cheeks, and I hop into the enclosure for a completely different reason —to wash away the memories.

It only takes a burst of cold water to wake me up.

"Shit!" I dart out of the freezing needles and slap at the taps to turn it warmer.

After a minute, I step back under the spray. My hair is a giant knot of a mess, and I grab the shampoo off the niche built into the tile and attempt to scrub it clean. Conditioner helps even more. Thankfully, the knot on my temple has gone down and no longer aches.

I rush through the process, not wanting an audience this morning, but when I turn off the water and spin around to reach for the door handle, Forge is already waiting.

Once again, he has a robe in his hands, and he's watching me intently.

With heat racing up my cheeks, I reach out to snatch the robe out of his grip. Using it to cover my body, I spin around and shove my soaking-wet arms into the sleeves, fighting as they get stuck.

Forge waits in silence as my emotions crush the walls I boxed them in with last night. Humiliation, betrayal, and anger rise as one like a phoenix from the ashes.

"I want a divorce." The words are out of my mouth before

I even realized that's what I planned to say, but Forge's stoic face is unreadable. "Did you hear me? I said I want a divorce."

Nothing. Not a hint of reaction. I wait for a response, but when nothing comes, I nod.

"Good talk. Glad that's done and we're on the same page." I sweep around him like I haven't a care in the world.

Forge's hand snaps out and wraps around my upper arm. "We're not done."

"Yes, we are. You lied to me. Played me. Tricked me. Whatever the hell you want to call it—and I'm done. Out. Finished. Go fuck yourself and play your games with someone else."

"I didn't lie to you."

My mouth drops open at his statement. "You had my sister kidnapped and then promised to rescue her if I married you! How is that not a lie?"

Forge's implacable expression hardens to stone. "De Vere is full of shit. I didn't have a fucking thing to do with your sister's kidnapping. You can think I'm the scum of the goddamned earth, but there are lines I refuse to cross. Hurting an innocent for my own gain is one of them."

I jerk my arm, trying to pull it from his grasp, but it's immovable. "What about me? I don't count as an innocent you hurt for your own gain?"

Forge releases his grip on me like I've suddenly burst into flames. "Did you, or did you not, bargain with me to secure your sister's freedom?"

I cross my arms over my chest and grit my teeth. "You already had a plan to get her back before I did! The timing is bullshit, Forge. Tell me you didn't know she'd been kidnapped when I told you. Tell me you didn't already have a rescue plan in place. I dare you to lie to my fucking face."

For long moments, I don't think he'll reply, but he finally does.

"I knew she'd been kidnapped before I left for Monte Carlo."

My jaw drops further at his admission. "See? You lied to me!"

"I didn't lie. I just didn't tell you what I knew, and you didn't ask."

"That's not fair. It's a lie of omission. You can split hairs all you want, but it doesn't change the fact that you tricked me into marrying you."

His nostrils flare as he takes a step toward me. "There was no trick. You agreed to a no-questions-asked deal. I told you I would benefit from it. You didn't ask how or why or when. Did you?"

"I was desperate!" I shout, and my screech echoes off the tile bathroom walls. "I would've done anything to save her."

"That's right. *Anything.* You just fucking said it, so stop pretending that I made you do something you weren't willing to do."

"Only if you promise me that you didn't have a fucking thing to do with Summer being taken." I jab him in the chest with a finger as his gaze smolders with anger.

Forge wraps a hand around my finger and gives it a squeeze. "I swear on the grave of the man who was the closest thing to a father I've ever known—I didn't have a goddamned thing to do with your sister's kidnapping. I might not be a good guy, but I'm not the fucking devil you want me to be either."

"Then who did it?" I demand as he releases his grip on me and steps back. "And don't even think about lying to me. I will tell the whole fucking world my side of the story if you do."

Forge's jaw tenses, and I wonder if my threat carries any

weight, or if it's just an annoyance he'll swat away like a fly. Without meeting my gaze, he replies.

"Your father has enemies."

The word throbs in my head like a heartbeat. *Father. Father. Father.* My stomach threatens to revolt.

"I don't have a father," I tell him as I rush out of the bathroom, wanting to run away from this discussion that I demanded happen.

"You weren't the immaculate conception, Indy. You have a father," Forge says as I march toward another door that I assume hides a closet.

I'm right, and it's full of men's clothes. I reach for the first T-shirt I spot and whip off the robe to pull it over my head. My hand brushes the cut on my side, and thankfully, it doesn't hurt anymore. Once I'm covered, I stomp out of the closet and go back to the bathroom to find my shorts from yesterday.

Forge stands in the bedroom, watching me come and go, but I don't face him again until I'm fully dressed and the T-shirt is knotted at one hip, like I'm making some kind of fashion statement instead of dressing out of desperation.

"Did you hear what I said?" he asks.

"My mother said he was dead. Why the fuck should I believe you instead?" I turn for the door, but Forge reaches out again to grasp my wrist.

"Did it ever occur to you that she might have lied?"

I spin around to face him. "What reason would she have?"

His flinty gray eyes study my face. I have no idea what he's looking for, but I know what I'm not getting out of him. Answers.

"I don't have a father. There's nothing you can do to make me believe you. I don't want to hear it." I tug my arm back and head for the door.

"Your father is the one who told me your sister had been kidnapped. He thinks the kidnappers thought they had you."

I freeze in place. *No. No. No. That's not possible.* While I rage against Forge's statement in my head, he continues.

"Did you ever give Summer one of your IDs? Did she ever tell you that she uses your name to get into poker games?"

My mouth drops open. *No. Fucking. Way.*

"She wouldn't."

"She has. She did. That's why they thought she was you."

I lift a hand to my mouth to cover my shock. As much as I want to scream that he's lying . . . I know my sister. It sounds exactly like something she would do. When she was sixteen, she swiped my ID to get into clubs and thought I wouldn't find out. *And she never fucking grew up because Alanna and I have coddled her.*

I look down at the chipped pink polish on my big toe as I try to process all of this.

"You're telling me that my sister pretended she was me and got kidnapped by an enemy of some guy who claims to be my father." It comes out as a statement, not a question, because I already believe him.

"Yes."

My stomach tumbles like someone tossed it in the spin cycle with the laundry. I turn around slowly and face Forge.

"And this guy just happened to come to you for help?" My voice shakes as I ask the question, because I know I won't like the answer.

"I'm a businessman. People come to me with requests."

"That doesn't tell me a goddamned thing."

Forge's gaze narrows on me. "Why should I tell you the truth now when you're planning on walking out that door in seconds regardless?"

My shoulders hike up around my ears. "I don't know. So you can fucking sleep at night or look yourself in the mirror?"

"I sleep just fine."

With my jaw tensing, I take a step toward him. "I'm done playing your game, Forge. I'm out."

"I'll make it worth your while to stay."

I blink twice, like it's somehow going to help me decide if he just said what I think he did. "You are not seriously trying to negotiate with me right now."

"I need something from you, and you want something from me. So, yes. This is a negotiation."

I shake my head and spin around to grab the door handle. "I'm not interested."

"Would you be interested for a hundred million dollars?"

My hand stills on the knob, and I blink at the wooden panel over and over. *Surely, I didn't hear him right.*

"What did you say?" I whisper.

"One hundred million dollars. I'll deposit it into your bank account in thirty days, and all you have to do is not file for divorce."

My fingers tingle. As much as my pride wants me to tell him to go to hell, a hundred million dollars is a lot of fucking money . . . and it turns out my pride can be bought.

Never accept the first offer. Play the man, not the game.

Slowly, I turn around and cross my arms over my chest. The T-shirt droops off one shoulder as I stare at the naked man before me.

"We didn't sign a prenup. If I divorce you, I'll get a hell of a lot more than a hundred million."

"We've been married for twenty-four hours. No judge is going to give you half of anything. Take the hundred million. It'll be the easiest money you've ever earned."

Fuck. He's probably right. A billionaire wouldn't get married without a prenup, regardless of some potential upside

that I still don't understand, if it could cost him half of everything. That would be stupid, and Forge is anything but.
Besides, I don't want half his businesses. I want enough cold,
hard cash never to have to worry about money for the rest of
my life.

I straighten my shoulders and lift my chin. "Fine. But I
want two hundred million, and not a penny less."

FORGE

*I*t takes everything I have not to smile. She's fucking magnificent, not to mention opportunistic and ruthless. I approve.

"One fifty," I counter.

"One seventy-five," she shoots back.

"Deal." I step forward and hold out my hand.

Indy's attention drops to my dick, which is also wide awake and rising to attention. Her gaze darts back to my face.

It's a good dick day. What can I say?

"Do you always shake on deals over"—she waves her hand toward my cock—"that situation?"

I don't know how it's possible, but I lose control of my lips and they curve into a smile. I shouldn't be surprised. This is what she does to me every damn time I'm around her . . . at least, when I'm not baring my teeth to chase someone else away from what's mine.

I wait another beat with my hand outstretched. "Rarely is anyone staring at my dick while they're shaking my hand."

"So you think." She forces her attention back to my face, then slides her hand into mine and squeezes it. "I bet there are plenty of people who've been dick-struck by the Kraken. But don't worry, I'll get over it. In thirty days, it'll just be one more dick in a long line of dicks I get to experience over the rest of my life."

My grip tightens around her hand as my smirk fades away, and I yank her closer to me. Indy tries to pull away, but I'm not letting her go yet. Not until she and I are very clear on the claw-like jealousy that grabbed hold of me.

"I'm only going to say this once. Regardless of the circumstances, you're my wife, and I don't share. Remember that, or I promise you won't enjoy the consequences."

Her blue eyes, now back to normal, widen at my quiet, low words.

"Am I understood?"

"Your hard-on is jabbing into me as you stake your claim on your property. I hear you, Forge. And just so *I'm* clear—I don't share either. You touch another woman, and I'll make sure the Kraken doesn't live to tell the tale. Not because I'm jealous, though." She pauses to clarify. "But because I don't need you making me look like a poor, cheated-on wife before this is all over. I do have a reputation to uphold."

"Fine. I agree."

She jerks her hand out of mine and steps back. "There's one more thing we need to agree on."

"What?"

"Our story. What we're going to tell people. How this started. How it ended."

I study her for a beat before I start with the truth. "I saw you. You fascinated me. I wanted you. You married me because of my . . ." I glance down at my dick. "Charm."

Indy's nostrils flare, and I know she wants to argue, but she doesn't. Probably because she's saving up to strike another blow.

"Fair enough, as long as we agree that publicly, everyone will know that *I'm* the one who ended it."

I narrow my gaze on her, inexplicably annoyed that I have to talk about how this is ending.

Why the fuck do I care? It was always going to end. There was never any other option. I just hadn't thought about it, and now that I'm getting to know her . . . it's not a subject I want to discuss.

"We'll deal with it when the time comes, in a manner that won't reflect badly on either of us," I tell her in my most bored businesslike tone.

She lifts her stubborn-as-hell chin. "Fine, but I'm still the one ending it."

My phone vibrates on the nightstand, saving me from having to respond.

"I believe that's our cue to meet our guests."

"What guests?" Panic widens Indy's eyes.

"I invited your mother and sister to brunch. I'm glad we've got our story straight. Keep it vague for Alanna. She doesn't need to know all the details."

INDIA

I don't like taking orders from him, especially when he's naked and I'm clothed. My concentration has been shot to shit, and I can't stop sneaking peeks at his dick.

Seriously, it should be illegal for a man to be that well-endowed and for a penis to be so attractive. It's like a lodestone, and I keep losing my train of thought because of the throbbing ache between my legs reminding me exactly how we spent last night.

From now on, I have to keep my legs closed and forget what he's able to do to my body.

I take back what I thought earlier. It was the drugs. There's no way he's really that good at giving orgasms, I tell myself. But then another part of my brain is already volunteering to put it to the test as soon as possible, just to rule out the possibility.

"Do you agree?" Forge says my name, and there's a hint of a smile in his tone, like he's reading my mind again.

"Agree?" I ask, having lost the thread of conversation.

"Eyes up here."

I try to ignore the smirk on his face when I look up. "Put

the damn thing away then if you don't want me to get distracted by it. It would be like me stripping naked and doing jumping jacks, and then yelling at you when you can't stop watching my tits bounce."

His smile widens. "I'm willing to try it, just to prove you wrong."

Wait, did he just *wink*? Asshole.

"Not happening. And yes, I agree. I'll tell Alanna whatever will keep her from asking too many questions and still let her leave with warm fuzzies, instead of knowing that I sold myself to the devil to save Summer when you were already bringing her back."

All levity flees the room at my words.

"You agreed to no questions asked," Forge says, and I cut him off with a middle finger.

"Just wait until you have to make a deal when you're desperate enough to agree to *no questions asked* terms."

With that, I use my incredible powers of avoidance, and I step around my massive naked husband and head for the door.

"And put some fucking clothes on before you scare everyone with that beast."

I slam the door behind me, blocking out the laughter that chases me into the hall.

"WE RODE IN A HELICOPTER! Never in my life did I expect to take a helicopter when a boat would do just as well."

Alanna's voice is full of awe and excitement as I hug her, and I let a little of the bitterness that still festers slide away.

"It picked us up right down at the quay," she says, "and everyone probably assumed we were famous."

"How was the ride?" I ask.

"Amazing, and he promised to take us on a tour and circle all of Ibiza on our way back."

I release her from the hug. "I'm so glad you enjoyed it."

Her expression turns serious as she looks from me to the sprawling white villa behind me. "Now, are you going to tell me how the hell you ended up married to Jericho Forge when you left on a jet with Bastien de Vere?"

As soon as she says Bastien's name, I whip around to make sure no one overheard it. "Let's not talk about him. He's what you'd call *persona non grata* here."

One of Alanna's silver brows goes up. "I was right. Forge is the jealous type, and when he saw you with Bastien, he realized he wasn't going to let that spoiled trust-fund brat have you, so he swept in to claim you for himself, and then rescued your baby sister because he couldn't possibly let the situation stand and cause you duress." Alanna sounds like she just rattled off the plot to one of the romance novels she devours by the stack every afternoon.

"Yes. Exactly. How did you guess?" I say, my tone bright and cheery.

Her expression turns skeptical as hell. "You expect me to believe that?"

"How about we all pretend that your story is the truth, and someday, a long, long time from now, when I'm a very wealthy divorcée, I'll tell you what actually happened."

"I don't like that plan, and from what I've gathered in the last eighteen hours, I have to assume this is somehow Summer's fault."

No one could ever accuse Alanna of being slow or dumb, so I should have expected that she would have already interrogated Summer and formed her own conclusions.

I meet Alanna's familiar gaze and give her as much honesty as I can. "I'm not at liberty to discuss the details, but you know I'll tell you more when I can."

She nods in understanding as my sister wanders back from where she dipped a foot in the pool. We both spear her with sharp looks.

"What? What did I do?"

A deep voice replies to her question, much to my surprise.

"Let's start with you impersonating your sister to get into underground poker games. That won't be happening again, will it, Ms. Baptiste?" Forge stops in front of the long table set for brunch on the patio, and I watch my sister's face.

"Please tell me you didn't."

"Jesus, great way to make brunch super awkward right out of the gate, *brother dearest*." Summer's tone is heavy on the sarcasm.

"Summer!" Alanna's tone is sharp with worry. "You told me you were working as an intern at fashion shows."

My sister tosses her blond hair over her shoulder in one of her signature defensive moves. "It's not like Indy didn't break every goddamned rule in the world to get into poker games when she was first starting out."

I raise my finger, but Forge speaks first.

"This isn't about Indy. She can do whatever the hell she wants. This is about you, pretending to be someone you're not, and putting yourself in situations that make your mother and sister worry. You won't be doing that again, will you, Summer?" Forge faces my sister, and not a single hint of his rigid posture invites argument.

Summer pops her hip and drops a hand on it. "Indy, are you seriously going to let him talk to me like that?"

I pretend to consider it for a moment before nodding like a bobblehead doll. "Yep, sure am. He's right. You fucked up. And what's more—*you were pretending to be me when you cheated and got caught.* Did you even think for one second how that would reflect on *my reputation* that you were trading on to get into the game?"

Summer's head jerks back. "What the hell are you talking about? I never cheated! And if I had, I sure wouldn't have gotten caught, because you taught me better than that. I didn't even get to play the game!"

A shroud of silence settles over all of us as we process Summer's admission.

My pulse beats in my ears as I realize they played me.

"They lied," I whisper. "The kidnappers . . . they lied to me."

I don't know why I'm so shocked. It's not like kidnappers are beacons of truth and honesty, but that changes everything. Especially because Bastien claimed the kidnapping was a setup and that Forge was behind it.

I turn and look at Forge, who's also staring at Summer with surprise lining his features. "Did you know . . ."

His lips flatten into a hard line. "We'll discuss this later." He glances at Summer. "You need to write down everything you remember from the moment you found out about the game you tried to play until the second you set foot in my chopper. Understood?"

She nods, her lighter blue eyes finally showing fear. My resilient, ballsy sister might have just given us a lead to help find out what the hell is really going on here. If Forge didn't set up the kidnapping . . . that means Bastien had to have been involved.

I'm going to find out every damn thing, and then I'm going to strangle him with my own bare hands.

"So, how about we have some brunch?" I say, forcing cheerfulness into my tone.

18

FORGE

"*E*nter," I call when someone knocks on the door to my office a few hours later.

The wooden panel swings open and Indy strides in, her hips swaying in a short green sundress that looks like it's meant to be casual, but on her, it emphasizes every curve of her body. She's wearing a pair of Adidas sneakers as well, which makes me assume her sister brought her clothes this morning. Part of me is annoyed because I would have happily kept her naked or wearing my clothes for as long as possible before I broke down and had something sent for her.

Yep. I'm fucked.

"We neglected a very important piece of our conversation earlier," Indy says. She sounds part sharp and partly mocking.

Actually, that may just be the special tone that she reserves for me. I must be fucked in the head, because it makes my dick hard.

"And what piece was that?" I ask, affecting boredom as I lean back in my chair and cross an ankle over my knee.

"I'm going to need an advance on that hundred seventy-five mil you owe me." She lifts her chin as if daring me to question her.

Which is exactly what I'm going to do.

I sit up. "What the hell for? You have a credit card. What else could you need?"

Indy crosses to my desk and plops into the chair across from it. She leans back, kicking her white sneakers up on the edge as she crosses her arms over her chest.

"You really think I'm just going to sponge off you for the next month? Sorry, Forge. That's not how I'm built. I work for my money. Always have, always will. Being married to you isn't going to change a damn thing about that."

Ah. Now I know what she wants.

"You're asking if I'll allow you to sit a game?"

A myriad of emotions cross her face, and it's not until the rage turns into a burst of laughter that I realize I've miscalculated with my words.

"*Asking if you'll allow me*? That's cute, Forge. Real cute. I don't know how your *arrangements* with your women worked in the past, but I'm going to lay out how things are going to work between us."

Her attitude doesn't help deflate my dick. As a matter of fact, all it does is make me want to bend her over my desk and fuck the sass right out of her.

"Is that right?"

She slides her feet off my desk and repositions herself to lean forward and plant both elbows on the antique wood. "I'm going to live my life and you're going to live yours. You don't bother me; I won't bother you."

"And if I don't agree?"

"Tough shit. Because I've got a game, and I'm gonna play it and win, which means I need a million in cash from you right now. Then I'll get out of your way, and you can go about your business."

I shake my head slowly. "That's not going to work for me, India."

19

INDIA

"*W*hat do you mean, that won't work for you?" My voice shoots up an octave, even though I promised myself I'd be assertive and calm and professional in order to secure what I want before getting the hell out of his presence, and I'm already losing the battle.

"We also neglected to discuss another very important point in our relationship." Forge uncrosses his legs and leans forward, matching my posture with both elbows on the desk. "Because I very much want to *bother you*, especially when you walk into my office with your attitude on high and that dress taunting me."

I look down at the green T-shirt dress I'm wearing with its ruched sides that help camouflage all my imperfections.

"Come here," he says, and I meet his serious gray stare.

"What? Why?"

Forge pushes away from the desk, spreads his legs, and points to the spot between them. "You want your million dollars? Come stand right here."

It's a trap. I already know it.

I plant my feet on the floor and grip the arms of the chair.

"That's not how this works. This isn't a negotiation. This is you giving me what you owe me."

The creases around his eyes deepen like he's amused. "Everything in life is a negotiation."

My lips pinch together. I don't want to give in, because at least with this massive wooden desk between us, I have an illusion of safety and distance. Proximity, I've learned, is my downfall when it comes to this enigmatic man I married.

"No."

He shrugs. "Fine. Good luck sitting a game with no stake."

"You're determined to make me hate you, aren't you?"

Something unreadable flashes across his features as he lifts his chin higher, like a goddamned pasha on a throne, waiting for the newest member of his harem to be introduced.

No, like a pirate king awaiting the presentation of the wenches he claims as his own booty.

No, Indy. Stop. No thinking about booty. The memories of how hard I came with his finger in my previously virgin ass rise to the surface, and my thighs tense of their own volition.

"Stubborn woman. You don't know how to bend, do you?" Forge's deep voice, normally rough, smooths into silk and wraps around me like a rope, tugging on my subconscious to bring me closer to doing his bidding.

"You don't want me to bend," I say. "You want a mindless doll that'll do whatever you say."

A light that's equally predatory and excited brightens Forge's gray eyes. "If I wanted blind obedience, I could have any number of women here within fifteen minutes who wouldn't question my orders."

I bare my teeth. "You agreed to no sharing."

His lips curve up with a knowing smile. "I did, indeed. And I don't want another woman. You lied to me when you claimed to be a lousy lay. I want to fuck you again, India, and I'm willing to make a deal so we both get what we want."

I shoot out of my chair. "I'm not a whore."

"We've already covered that. Now, come here if you want to leave this island—at all—in the next thirty days."

Rage propels me around the desk. "You can't fucking keep me here against my will. I—"

Whatever I was about to say is cut off when Forge's hands wrap around my hips and yank me off-balance to land over his knees.

"Hey!" I screech, but his palm lands on my ass with a stinging strike.

"You've got an attitude that makes my dick as hard as a rock."

"Go fuck yourself—"

Another swat lands on my other cheek, and the burn sends heat and wetness blooming between my legs.

I should hate his high-handed behavior. I should want to murder him, but my body doesn't care about *should*. It only knows how damn good it feels. My hips arch against my will, and I lift, seeking the next strike from his hand.

"Fuck, you tempt me, India."

Another strike lands, and then another. I can't help but rock against him, seeking the contact on my clit that it'll take to get me off. Forge's wide hand strokes over the fabric of my dress, caressing where he spanked, and all my nerve endings light up.

I want to beg him to keep going, push up my dress, and get me off, but my stubbornness keeps me silent.

"This ass . . ." Forge cups my burning cheek and squeezes. "It belongs to me. You sit at a table and play a game, you do it knowing that you come home *to me* when you're done. Do you understand?"

I push against his thighs again, and instead of keeping me deliciously trapped, he helps me rise to my feet beside him.

He's still a fucking caveman.

"If you're going to work a girl up, the least you can do is finish her off."

He shakes his head. "No. I want you thinking about exactly what you want from me, even if you won't admit it."

I grit my teeth together, hating that he knows exactly how he affects me. I cross my arms over my chest and pop my hip.

"Fine. Now, where's my money? Oh, and by the way, I'm taking the chopper. I am Mrs. Forge, after all, aren't I?"

20

FORGE

*T*hree hours later, I watch the chopper hover over the blue water holding three of the most trusted members of my security team, and a woman who probably wouldn't cry at my funeral if I got pushed off a cliff. More than likely, she'd be the one to shove me over.

India wasn't supposed to affect me like this. She wasn't supposed to get under my skin and into my blood. She wasn't supposed to entertain me and challenge me.

We all know how that worked out.

Now she's on her way to a game in Mallorca. Every instinct tells me I should have gone with her, but I couldn't. A very important visitor will arrive here in two hours, and India's not ready to meet her father yet. Not by a long shot.

Grigory Federov won't be happy either when he realizes the daughter he's expecting to be reunited with isn't here. But that's my choice. I refuse to spring something like this on her before she's ready. For now, I'd rather face his wrath alone.

Especially when he finds out that I didn't just find his daughter . . .

I married her.

*F*orge's ego knows no bounds. I'm settled between three hulking men, all of whom look like former black-ops types who kill people for fun and hide bodies in their spare time.

I've nicknamed them Batman, Spiderman, and Superman in my mind, because I was arguing about not needing any kind of security when Forge told me their names, and now I feel like too much of an asshole to ask after the fact since I already forgot them. I mean, they should be flattered, right? They're the best superheroes the comic-book world has to offer.

When we land on Mallorca, I reach for the small duffel bag at my feet, but Superman, who wears a royal-blue shirt beneath his dark suit, grabs it for me.

"I'll carry that for you, Mrs. Forge."

Hearing him address me by that name is strange as hell, but I suppose that's who I am now. And since I'm already basking in the luxury that comes with the title, I might as well own it.

"I should've been comped a room at the casino."

Spiderman, the youngest-looking of the three who gives off Peter Parker vibes, nods. "We've secured the penthouse, and Mr. Forge directed his assistant to have a hairstylist, makeup artist, and personal shopper meet you upon your arrival."

Mr. Forge did what?

I look at Spiderman like he lost his damn mind along with his Spidey sense. "Excuse me?"

"Mr. Forge wanted to make sure you had everything you needed."

That shouldn't send a whoosh of lust through me, but of course my traitorous body doesn't listen.

"Is he planning on making some kind of grand entrance, and he wants me to be properly outfitted on his arm?"

Spiderman shakes his head. "No, ma'am. He has a business meeting and won't be leaving the island tonight."

"Who is he meeting with?" My mind riots, thinking of him having a cozy dinner for two with that bitch Juliette.

"I'm afraid I don't know, but Mr. Forge prefers to meet in his own territory."

Of course he does.

I bite down on my lip and take a deep breath. *Forge made the stipulation about not sharing. He didn't just spank me, hand me a million dollars, and send me on my way so he could get a piece of ass. I don't care who he's meeting. I will not let my brain psych me out. I'm here to work.*

I paste a smile on my face before I speak again. "Wonderful. Then there's no chance of my concentration being disturbed tonight." I look at each man's face. "Which means . . . I would be forever in your debt if all three of you could figure out how to do your job without making it look like you're doing your job."

"But, Mrs. Forge—"

When Batman, the guy dressed in all black with a Bruce

Wayne look about him, tries to chime in, I silence him with a raised finger.

"I swear I'm not trying to make your life harder. I know you have orders. I get it. But I'm here to outplay and out-bluff every man at the table, and I can't do that while you're hovering over my shoulder. There has to be some middle ground that we can all live with, because I need to win tonight."

Because I can't be dependent on Forge for every nickel and dime I want to spend, I add silently to myself.

Each man nods, but only Superman replies.

"Understood, Mrs. Forge."

"Are you sure? Because I can't have any of you looking like you're working as a team and sending signals to one another or to me. If you do, I'll be tossed out on my ass for being a cheater. My reputation will go to shit, and I'll never get to sit a decent game again. That's a chance I can't take. Understand?"

This time, I get three "yes, ma'am" responses in unison.

"Glad we're clear," I tell them with a blindingly bright smile.

The pilot signals the tower that we're landing, and I glance out the window as we approach.

"It's time to go kick ass and make money."

22

FORGE

*G*rigory Federov arrives in a black helicopter that appears to be civilian, but it looks like it could easily morph into a gunship capable of leveling the entire island.

One has to wonder if he flies it for intimidation or out of necessity.

Either way, I'm grateful not to be his enemy . . . at least for the time being. There's no guarantee this meeting is going to end with us both working toward a common goal, but I'm hopeful he can be persuaded to see my side of things.

Indy is playing to win tonight, and so am I.

As soon as the chopper lands on the helipad, Federov climbs out, followed by two men dressed in black suits. The rotor wash flips his thinning silver hair from side to side as he strides toward me. He's seventy-four but doesn't look a day over sixty. According to my sources, he target-shoots from horseback whenever possible, and frequently uses pictures of business rivals for bull's-eyes. His tailored suit jacket fits his stocky frame well, but his collar is already open and his tie is gone. Fair enough, because I hate wearing a tie as well.

His gaze travels over my shoulder as he comes to a stop before me, no doubt looking for his daughter. My suspicions are confirmed when the first words leave his mouth.

"Where is she?"

"She's not here."

"What do you mean, she's not here?" The lines on his tanned face deepen with his scowl. "You said you found my daughter. I come to take her home, and now you say she is not here. Is this how you do business, Forge? You lure people with false promises? I want to see her!" His accent thickens as his emotions rise.

I need to defuse the situation before he stalks back to his chopper and never answers another one of my calls again—or he orders his henchmen to shoot me. Goliath would snipe them both before they could, but I really hope to end this meeting without bloodshed.

To that end, I pull my phone from my pocket and push the button to wake it up. The lock screen is a picture of India standing on the deck of my yacht, taken from above when she didn't know I was watching her.

"Here. Look. She's fine."

The old man reaches out with surprising speed and snatches the phone from my hands to stare at the screen in awe. "She looks just like my Irina." The twinkle of nostalgia fades from his blue eyes as fast as it appeared. "Where is she now? I want to take her home."

"She'll be home tomorrow morning."

"This isn't her home." He waves an arm around at Isaac's island. "Her home is Russia."

"Her home is wherever she wants it to be. You're not dealing with a child, Mr. Federov. Your daughter is a head-strong woman who doesn't take orders well."

"She will adjust," he says stubbornly, like it's a decree.

"No, Federov, she's not going to adjust. She's not going anywhere with you."

He stares at me in confusion, as if he can't quite understand that I'm telling him he won't get his way.

If India were standing with us right now, I would tell her that this is a big part of why I married her. *No Russian is going to bulldoze my wife.* Only I get to do that.

"She is my daughter. She will do as I say."

I smile at him. "She's my wife, Federov. That means you deal with me."

23

INDIA

*W*hen I walk into the high-stakes poker area of Mallorca's most exclusive casino, I feel different. Maybe because I arrived via helicopter, was whisked up to my suite, met by my glam squad, and was then escorted down with one bodyguard ahead of me carrying my chips and two trailing behind in an attempt at looking innocuous.

So this is what it feels like to be a billionaire. Or at least the wife of one. I'm not complaining.

The men standing around the table that has been set up for our game stare as I approach. My sapphire-blue dress hugs my curves and is going to be the perfect distraction. I can't help but wonder what orders Forge gave the personal shopper. Somehow, I doubt it was *buy something that will have the men looking at her tits and not their cards.* But with this dress, that's exactly what the outcome will be, and I'm not complaining about that either.

"Ms. Baptiste, it's a pleasure to have you at our game." Julio Gallardo, the game's organizer and the source of my invitation, steps forward and offers a hand. I shake it and can't help but think that it's smooth and womanly compared to Forge's strong, calloused grip.

Why am I thinking about him? I'm here to play. I can't help it, though.

Forge has been on my mind every second while I was getting ready, because he arranged for all of it without my knowledge. If another man had done that, I'd say it was sweet and thoughtful, but I'm still trying to figure out Forge's angle. *But I'm not letting that distract me from my game.*

"The pleasure is all mine, I assure you," I say to Julio as he releases my hand. "Thank you for the invitation."

He steps away, and I catch sight of a familiar face just beyond him.

"Mr. Belevich, I didn't expect to see you here."

The Russian I played against the night I lost to Forge eyes me. "Ms. Baptiste. I do hope your luck has not yet returned."

I keep my well-practiced fake smile in place. "I suppose we'll see, sir."

"Like you'd have a chance to beat her on even her worst day, Belevich."

I freeze at the mocking words coming from behind me. *Bastien.* I turn toward him slowly, denying the urge to touch the knot on my head from his stupid boat.

What the fuck? He has a black eye and his shoulders aren't quite square, like he's nursing some kind of injury I can't see.

"What the hell happened to you?" I ask.

"I ran into a door," Bastien deadpans.

Was Forge the door? No. He couldn't have been. *Goliath, maybe?* He was only a minute behind us when we climbed into the chopper, or so I thought.

"You should be more careful," I tell him, and we both know I mean he should stay the hell away from me.

One corner of his mouth curls. "Maybe you should take

your own advice." He glances behind me. "But then again, I suppose your bodyguards take care of any doors in your path."

Okay, now this conversation is turning cryptic, and I don't have time for distractions. Focus on the game, Indy.

"I didn't expect to see you playing tonight," I say carefully, my tone measured and even.

"I'm not playing. I'm just here for the entertainment," he says with his trademark smug smile, and I can't help but wonder what the hell I'm missing.

Something about this feels . . . off.

"Enjoy the entertainment, then." Wanting to put as much space between Bastien and me as possible, I turn back to Gallardo and ask for an introduction to another player I've not yet met.

"Of course, Ms. Baptiste, I'd be happy to introduce you to—"

"It's Mrs. Forge now, Gallardo," Bastien says, interrupting. "You wouldn't want to accidentally offend your favorite billionaire by calling his wife by the wrong name, would you?"

Gallardo's dark eyebrows shoot up to his receding hairline at the announcement. "Mr. Jericho Forge?"

Fucking Bastien. Of course he had to go there.

"Yes, Forge took a wife. Shocking, isn't it?" Bastien grins broadly, and I hope it strains his black eye, because now Belevich is staring at me intently as well.

Fabulous. Just fabulous.

"Congratulations, Mrs. Forge. I'll have the server fetch a bottle of champagne so we can toast your nuptials," Gallardo says, and I smile sweetly at him.

"Actually, I'm ready to play." I gesture to the table. "Gentlemen, shall we?"

We select chairs, but before I take mine, Bastien stops at

my side. Batman takes a step toward me from across the room, but I hold up a finger to halt his movement.

I face Bastien. "If I were you, I'd stay far, far away from me."

"Good luck, Indy," he says with an enigmatic expression. "You're going to need it. And I'm not talking about the game."

24

FORGE

$\mathcal{F}$rom the way Federov goes through the contract, line by line, scratching things out and scribbling in the margins, you'd think he's never seen it before in his life, which isn't the case. Page after page, he slides them across my desk, each one changed in some way.

I read over the revisions and make a list of counterproposals on the notepad beside me. I haven't done business like this in years, maybe ever. But sometimes, when you reach that upper echelon, billionaires do things the old-fashioned way.

Hell, if I'd turned India over to Federov, there's a hell of a good chance that he would have agreed to my deal with just a handshake and nothing else. His irritation and the number of changes he's making are in direct proportion to his anger at being thwarted from seeing his daughter tonight.

When he reaches the end, he pushes the final piece of paper across my desk. "When you agree to all of those changes, then I will consider signing your deal."

I scan the remaining sheet for his objections before adding it to the stack. "You realize you've completely reversed several of your positions that we negotiated previously."

Federov leans back in the chair and crosses his arms over his chest, reminding me enough of his daughter to be uncanny. "Because we made a deal and then you changed things. I will not let you manipulate me, Forge."

I rest my elbows on the arms of my chair and lace my fingers together in my lap. "Sir, under any other circumstance, I wouldn't hesitate to manipulate you in every possible way to achieve my aims."

The Russian's stare intensifies, and I'm lucky he left his bodyguards outside the room. "Why would you tell me this?"

"Because this is a completely different situation than I normally find myself in, and I'm trying not to manipulate either of you more than necessary. In fact, your daughter doesn't want to know anything about you. As far as she's concerned, you don't exist, which is exactly what she was raised believing."

Federov's nostrils flare as he jerks forward and slaps a hand on my desk. "This is not my fault!"

"And it's not her fucking fault either," I say, my voice dropping into a growl. "I have to make the right decision for her too, because she's . . . she's . . ." I trail off, trying to think of how to describe the most complex and intriguing woman I've ever met in my life.

Federov lifts his chin and narrows his gaze. "Why did you marry my daughter, Forge?"

I look down at the papers in front of me and push them into a neat stack, not sure how the hell to answer that question. "Because it made sense."

He shakes his head, his lips parting like he's just realized something crucial. He lifts his hand and points at me across the desk. "You wanted an advantage over me, and maybe even to protect her, though she does not need protecting. But now . . . now I think the reason you are keeping her from me is something else. It is not only business anymore. This is personal now."

I press my lips together, not ready to have this conversation with Grigory Federov now . . . or preferably ever.

"What do you want to hear, Federov? That I have an attachment to her that has nothing to do with business? Is that going to change your mind somehow?"

His faded blue eyes twinkle, and I can't help but assume that's the color Indy's will likely be in fifty years.

Federov uncrosses his arms and sits back, his posture shifting from aggressive to relaxed. "I should have expected no less from a daughter of my loins. Only such a woman could throw the mighty Jericho Forge off his coldblooded negotiations."

At first, I think his words carry a note of mockery, but they don't. It's *pride*.

"She's an extraordinary woman."

"Of course she is. She descends from the blood of nobles . . . one of whom was so entranced by his servant girl that he made her his wife. My Illyana could charm me into giving her whatever she wanted at three years old. She was the heart of my heart. And when she was taken from me by that deceitful whore, my heart failed to beat again until the day I heard she might still live."

Federov pauses, his gaze focused on nothing for a moment before returning to me. "Whatever you think I have planned for my daughter, Mr. Forge, it is not in bad faith. I am an old man. I am sick. My days are numbered. In fact, I would not have picked you as a husband for Illyana because they say you want nothing but revenge."

He regards me for a few seconds before he continues. "But my Illyana has changed you already. Perhaps . . .

perhaps all is as it should be. Who am I, at this age, to question what fate has in store?"

I study the old man's features, looking for evidence of the illness he just admitted to, but I see no signs. Whatever it is that ails him, he still carries himself with pride, and his ox-like build hasn't lost enough of its bulk to raise concerns.

"How many people know you're ill?" I ask, hoping I don't offend the man.

"Very few. In my world, when they know you are weak, the vultures begin to circle, waiting to pick your bones clean."

Which is exactly my concern. "Who stands to gain the most from your death?"

Federov's gaze sharpens on me. "My daughter will inherit everything."

It's the answer I expected, but it won't help me protect her. "Who else? If she hadn't been found or didn't survive you . . . then who?"

His lips flatten as he considers. "I know what you are asking, but you do not need to worry. The threat to my Illyana's life has been handled. The man behind the kidnapping has been identified and eliminated."

There's not a single doubt in my mind that the man was not just *identified and eliminated.* He was probably tortured until he wished for a bullet to the brain. And yet, I still can't rest easy. Someone always has a motive.

"Are you certain?"

The Russian's brow dips. "Do not question me about such things. I am Russian. I handled it. The threat is no longer."

I brush my knuckles along the stubble of my jaw. "You're willing to bet your daughter's life on that?"

"You are falling in love with my daughter, Mr. Forge. That is why you will not believe me when I tell you she is as safe as I can keep her without having her by my side. You are lucky that I do not make her a widow right now for the way you went about securing her."

The death threat, handled with such nonchalance, isn't what makes me sit straighter. It's the other statement he made with such certainty. "*You are falling in love with my daughter.*"

How the hell would he know? What would make him think that?

When I don't reply, his knowing smile grows.

"You do not see it yet, Forge. But you will. Trust me. Russians feel things more intensely, even if we are trained not to show it. Now, get the vodka. We shall toast to the Federov line being continued, even if it has to be mixed with your American blood."

INDIA

*T*he stacks of chips rise and fall as the game progresses. Belevich's play is shrewder and smarter tonight, but I'm still better. I let him think he out-bluffed me on two early hands, strictly to lull him into a false sense of superiority. The other men at the table were strangers to me hours ago, but not anymore.

It's one thing that has always fascinated me about poker —you can sit down at a table with people you've never seen before in your life, and by the end of the game, you may know some of them more intimately than most people in their lives. At least, that's the way it works for me.

Read the man, play the man . . . and then I lure him in and take his money using everything I learn. That's how I earned the ridiculous name Queen Midas, when in reality, there's nothing magic about it. It's truly a simple equation that has always worked for me—until I played Jericho Forge.

If there were a real-life King Midas, it would be him.

I've never let a man's sheer presence send me into a tail-spin the way his did. He sent all my senses spiraling, and I played like I didn't have a single iota of skill or strategy that night. *How could I be so affected by a man?*

Looking back on the last week, I shouldn't be surprised at all how he affected me at the game. *Jericho Forge is not a normal man.*

How else could he have possibly gotten me to bet myself at the table, make me lose, tempt me with a million dollars, not kill me when I double-crossed him, but *marry me* instead —and then finally tell me it's all because I'm a means to an end because of the man who brought me into this world.

My father.

I shake off the thought, because if I go any deeper down that rabbit hole, my concentration will suffer, and I'm winning tonight.

The waiter comes around taking drink orders, but I wave him off. I have water, and that's all I need. As a rule, I never drink while I play because I don't want to risk losing my wits.

Belevich orders a vodka, which is typical for him. I've counted the drinks he's already had tonight, and this is number six. Maybe it's true what they say about Russians and vodka—that it's like mother's milk and doesn't affect them at all.

His play hasn't changed enough for me to think he's drunk, but with each drink, his attention fixates on me more and more. It's almost as if he's forgotten about the other three men at the table. Something burns in his icy blue eyes that I can't quite describe, but I refuse to let it unsettle me.

He tries to goad me into betting a bit more than I normally would for this hand, but I'm impervious to that kind of peer pressure anymore. And when the time comes to show our cards . . . *I win again.*

Belevich's broad forehead creases with lines of frustration. "You have the luck of the devil with you tonight, *Mrs.*

Forge. I suppose it only seems right, as you're now the devil's mistress."

I'm not exactly sure how to reply to that comment, but whatever the Russian needs to say to salvage his masculine pride is fine with me.

I rise halfway off my chair to sweep the stacks of chips in the center of the table toward me. "I'm just playing like I always play, Mr. Belevich."

"You didn't play this way last time. I suppose it was because your skill was muddied by your concern for your sister."

Startled, I knock the chips over. They spill toward me as my head jerks up to meet Belevich's stare. "What did you say?"

He sprawls in his chair, sipping his vodka, like he's finally got the advantage over me. And maybe he does, because *there's no way he should know anything about my sister.*

"I heard Little Sister had some trouble and needed Big Sister to bail her out with a chunk of cold, hard cash. But that's no longer an issue, clearly."

Blood roars in my ears as my mind spins. *Did Belevich have something to do with Summer's kidnapping?* Did he know about the game she planned to play? Did he know who arranged for her to be taken?

The only thing I want to do right now is jump out of my seat, march around the table, and drag him away by the hairs of his beard to question him, but I force myself to sit and arrange my chips like there's not a single thing on my mind other than winning this game. Belevich caught me off guard with his bomb, and I'm not going to let him see me falter more than he already has.

Whatever he knows can wait until we're not flanked by two Spaniards and a Frenchman, whose glances dart from me to Belevich like we're more interesting than the cards the dealer shuffles.

"How about we continue this discussion after the game, sir?"

Belevich salutes me with his vodka glass. "I look forward to it, Mrs. Forge."

FORGE

"*T*hank you for your hospitality, sir."

Grigory Federov and I stand a few yards from his chopper as the pilot starts the engine. I extend my hand, and he grasps it in a firm grip.

"You're welcome anytime. I just need to give India—"

He interrupts to correct me. "Illyana."

I want to tell him that I can't call her by that name because there's no way in hell she'll ever answer to it, but instead, I rephrase. "I need to give *your daughter* notice and see if she'll consent to meeting you."

"She will consent, or there will be no deal," he says as he straightens his shirtsleeves, as though he's oblivious to the fact that refusing to sign the deal will cost him hundreds of millions in lost profit. "I return to Saint Petersburg in the morning to attend to matters that cannot be postponed. I will tell you when to bring her there. She will see me there, in her home, and it will help her remember who she is."

And India will win every hand she ever plays with a royal flush, I finish in my head, because the odds are about the same.

However, if he wants to believe it, I'm not going to crush his hopes right now. No, I have to find a way to give him what he wants and close the deal . . . without doing something that will ensure my wife will hate me for the rest of my life. That's a consequence I'm no longer willing to risk.

I give Federov a nod. "I'll see what I can do."

"You will do it, Forge. I have no doubt. You like money more than anything, although perhaps . . . perhaps you are learning that it is not everything. You cannot take it with you when you go, and it makes for a lonely bedmate, as does revenge."

I tuck my hands into my pockets, watching a satisfied expression spread over the cagey old man's face. "You've mentioned revenge twice now, Federov. Exactly how much do you know about me?"

The Russian grins, and it's the first genuine smile I've seen on his face since he stepped foot on Isla del Cielo.

"Now? I know everything, Mr. Forge. Including the fact that not all things are as they appear. Be careful. I would hate to see my daughter a widow before you have proven your merit as a husband."

"I'm not worried, Federov." I incline my head at him as he turns toward the chopper. "Take care."

He salutes me and then walks toward the open door with his chin high, shoulders straight, and the slightest hint of a limp. I need absolutely zero convincing to believe with certainty that Indy is his daughter, and clearly, neither does he.

As the chopper lifts off the ground, I watch it fly away into the dark night sky, the lights dimming as it heads toward mainland Spain.

Grigory Federov is a juggernaut determined to get his own way. Unfortunately for him, I'm equally determined, and the most important negotiation of my life is no longer with him . . . it's with his daughter.

27

INDIA

"*C*ongratulations, Mrs. Forge. You played impressively tonight," Gallardo says as Batman collects my trays of chips.

"She did, indeed." Belevich rises from the table and approaches me as Batman steps away. "Which is why I want another chance to play you."

I meet Belevich's icy gaze, which remains sharp, even with the vodka he's been swilling all night. My mind is still grappling with his statement earlier about my sister. *How could he know?*

Batman pauses and looks at me. "Mrs. Forge, would you like us to escort you back to your room?"

"Give me five minutes, please," I tell him with a tight smile. I'm not leaving until I hear what Belevich has to say, because if there's a chance he was involved with Summer's kidnapping, I need to know. And I still haven't forgotten about the Russian men Miguel said were sniffing around my apartment.

When Batman continues to hover near the edge of the

dais where the poker game took place, I glance over at him. "I'll join you by the cashier shortly."

"Ma'am—"

"Thank you so much."

I know he's probably under orders not to leave my side, but I refuse to be babysat like I'm a child instead of a grown woman. Nothing is going to happen to me in this casino, except for perhaps someone trying to steal my winnings.

Or . . . The hair that has been standing on end all night as Bastien watched the game from the craps table comes back with a vengeance. I turn around to see that he's no longer there.

"De Vere has removed himself to the bar, Mrs. Forge," Belevich says, and my gaze cuts to him before searching for the familiar blond head of hair at the end of the bar.

Bastien's on his cell, and he's staring just as intently as he did throughout the game when I'd give in to my instincts to check. Bastien is no longer the playboy trying to sleep with me to prove he can. No, now he's the enemy, and I can practically see the rage rolling off him. Broke and desperate equals dangerous as hell in my book.

"How did you know who I was looking for?" I ask Belevich point blank.

Between him studying me like a pinned butterfly during the game and dropping hints that he has information about my sister, I can only draw one conclusion—Belevich has motives that I don't yet understand, and I need to treat him with caution.

Batman removed himself with my chips, but Spiderman isn't far away. Superman is nowhere to be seen. *It's fine. I'm safe. No one is going to get me here.* Unless my biggest threat is the man standing directly in front of me.

"De Vere has made no secret of his interest in you."

Belevich's reply tells me nothing, but it's not the information I'm really seeking anyway. "Who told you about my sister's *trouble*? Do you know who was involved?"

He shows absolutely no reaction to any of my questions and says nothing.

"Seriously?" I plant a hand on my hip. "If your poker face was that good during the game, Belevich, maybe I wouldn't always know when you're bluffing."

The taunt works, and the Russian scowls at me. "You are just as arrogant as your husband. I'm surprised he let you out of his sight. He doesn't seem like a man who would let his property off the leash, let alone off his little island."

I drop my head back and look up at the chandeliers and laugh. "Oh, I get it. You still think we live in a time when men own women and they have no say. So very backward of you."

Instead of biting back at me, Belevich smirks, holding his vodka glass carelessly in one hand. "But isn't that what they were going to do with your sister? Sell her off to a man to be his property?"

All humor evaporates from my entire body, and I stiffen. "What the fuck did you have to do with it, Belevich? I swear to Christ, I will fucking kill you myself if you—"

"Ah, Mrs. Forge. *Indy*," he says, his patronizing tone grating on me. "You assume too much. Rumors spread quickly in our crowd."

I grit my teeth, knowing I won't get a straight answer out of him tonight. "If you had something to do with any of this, be aware—I will find out and I will make you pay."

"You have a temper that would make your father very proud," he says as he raises the glass to his lips. "As long as he did not catch the sharp side of your tongue."

The statement catches me off guard, and I don't have time to school my reaction. Instead, I blurt, "You know my father?"

"Everybody knows Grigory Federov," Belevich says over his vodka.

Grigory Federov. I repeat the name silently before meeting Belevich's gaze again. "How long have you known who I am?"

He purses his lips and considers. "Long enough to form a hypothesis that ended up being very financially beneficial to me."

The phrase *financially beneficial* threatens to make my head explode, but I push it aside and try to fit the pieces of the puzzle together.

"You were the one who told him that I could be the long-lost daughter, weren't you?"

Belevich shrugs. "When you abandon your ploys and go in for the kill, you play like him. Bold. Aggressive. Out for blood. He would be proud to know this."

"You didn't answer my question."

His expression turns serious again. "I want to win my money back from you."

The abrupt change in conversation leaves me struggling to figure out what the hell his angle is, and what he really wants from me.

"Too late. Game's over."

"Not now," Belevich says with a shake of his head. "Next week. The Prague Grand Prix. We'll play again at the final table."

I know the game he references well. I won it years before in an upset they still talk about at the tables. It caught the attention of the people who needed to know I existed, and helped me cement my career as a professional poker player. I don't need to play it again. I have nothing to prove.

"I'm not interested," I tell him, shifting on my heel as though ready to leave.

"Of course, the pot isn't big enough to pique your attention. Why don't we make it more interesting?"

"How?"

"Five-million-dollar side bet."

He tosses it out like it's off the cuff, but I have to believe Belevich has been thinking about this throughout the game. *Why, though?* Instead of asking the question I really want answered, I taunt him.

"I'm married to a billionaire. Your five million doesn't even get my blood pumping," I say, injecting my tone with a bored note.

"What if I promised, win or lose, I will give you all the information I've been told about your sister?"

Abandoning my intent to stroll away and tell him to fuck off, I step closer into Belevich's personal space. "Why don't you just tell me now and we can skip this bullshit?"

I want to slap the half smile off Belevich's face as he speaks.

"Because I'm Russian and stubborn, and I want another chance to win my money back."

"I'll give you every fucking penny I won tonight."

He shakes his head. "It is not the same. I do not want you to give me anything. *I want to take it from you.*"

My jaw clenches, and a vein throbs in my temple. "Why Prague?"

"Because everyone will be watching, and they'll all cheer when I win."

Fucking men and their egos. I'm not going to get anything out of him tonight, except maybe . . . maybe I can get a little reassurance.

"I'll only consider it under one condition," I tell him.

He inclines his head as if waiting for me to continue.

"Is Summer still in danger?"

The Russian presses his lips together. "I would never

assume that you or anyone you love is completely safe, especially not now when you've married a man with many enemies who would love to see him brought low." He lifts his chin in the direction beyond my right shoulder. "De Vere is only one such enemy."

Great. More riddles.

I glance over my shoulder to where Bastien is still on the phone, eyeballing me and Belevich. Now, the only thing I want more than information is to get the fuck out of here, right now.

"If an invite to the grand prix shows up in my hand, I'll consider it. I make no promises."

"You'll get the invitation. I look forward to seeing you there." He lifts his vodka in salute before backing away and disappearing into the crowd beyond the dais.

Batman crosses over to me as soon as Belevich is out of sight. "Mrs. Forge, are you ready?"

"Yes, but I'm not staying here tonight. I want to pack my stuff and get the hell out of here."

"Yes, ma'am." Batman pulls his phone from his pocket. "I'll contact the pilot and pick up your winnings." Glancing at the other two guards, he says, "They'll escort you to your room, and we will arrange to depart as soon as possible."

"Thank you."

With two bodyguards trailing me, I stride past where Bastien sits at the bar, still on his cell phone. His gaze trails over me, leaving a creepy feeling in its wake.

What the hell are you scheming about now?

*I*nstead of guiding me to my hotel room to pack my bag and then taking me to the helipad, Superman and Spiderman lead me out of the back entrance of the casino as Spiderman returns his phone to his pocket.

"What's going on?" I ask as the door opens to reveal a black SUV. "Why aren't we taking the helicopter?" All my uneasy feelings rise to the surface as I stare at the unknown vehicle.

"We had a slight mechanical issue with the helicopter during refueling," Spiderman says. "The mechanic can't check it for several hours. Mr. Forge made other arrangements to get you home."

The mention of my husband calms my nerves a little. Regardless of whether I trust him, I don't believe he would put me in danger.

"How are we getting home?" I ask as Superman opens the door for me.

"Mr. Forge has a boat at the marina here. It won't be as quick as the chopper flight, but you'll be home as fast as possible."

I slide into the middle seat of the SUV, mulling over the last-minute complications, and I can't help but wonder if Bastien or Belevich are involved.

"Was the chopper tampered with?" I ask as Batman exits the casino, my bag in hand.

"No, ma'am. There's no sign of anything like that," Superman replies. "We could fly, but Mr. Forge's instructions were not to take any chances with your safety."

Warmth curls in my chest at his statement. "I hope you told Mr. Forge that I'm coming back with a big fat bag of money too."

Superman smiles. "I'll let you tell him that, ma'am."

"Fair enough. Let's go."

A FEW HOURS LATER, someone touches my arm.

"You're home," a deep voice whispers, interrupting my dream.

And it was a good dream too. One where a pirate boarded my ship, carried me off, and claimed me as his. I want to get back to it.

"Tired. Let me sleep."

"All right, Ace. You sleep."

FORGE

I lift my wife into my arms and carry her off the boat and up to the house. She's completely out, and curls against me like there's no question that I'll carry her where she needs to go and get her there safely.

"You're falling in love with my daughter."

I can't stop thinking about the Russian's claim. I've never been in love. Never had an interest in it. But now, I can't help but wonder if what I'm feeling about India is more than possessiveness and protectiveness.

It doesn't matter.

But the Russian . . . he seemed to think it did.

Regardless, now isn't the time to worry about it.

When we reach the house, Bates holds up a duffel bag. "What would you like me to do with this one, sir?"

"What's in it?"

"Your wife's winnings."

A smile curves my lips. "Put it on my desk. I'll lock it in the safe for her."

"Yes, sir." He turns to leave and then pauses. "Debrief in the morning, sir?"

I look down at the sleeping woman in my arms. "Yes. Everything else can wait."

He gives me another nod and moves toward my office.

I enter the bedroom and lay Indy down on her side of the bed. It's the one she's claimed, and regardless of the fact that it was my preferred side, I let her keep it.

That doesn't mean I'm in love with her.

Indy flops to her side, struggling against the fabric of the dress.

Considering how it clings to her body like a second skin, I can imagine why she'd want to be free. The zipper starts at the top of her back, and I slide it down until the material loosens. Carefully, I roll the dress down her body, only to realize she wore nothing beneath it.

When I free her legs, she's completely and beautifully naked. More than anything, I want to flip her onto her back and bury myself between her legs, fucking us both into oblivion, where I no longer have the brainpower to consider her father's words.

But I don't.

I reach for the covers to tuck her in and back away slowly.

*L*ight streams in from open curtains, waking me from the final and most delicious dream I've had all night.

My entire body tenses with panic for a moment when I remember I fell asleep on a boat, but nothing's rocking anymore.

Warmth radiates from a massive heat source beside me. A heavy arm hangs over my side, and morning wood presses against my ass.

I glance over my shoulder and bite down on my lip when I see the mess of dark hair shielding Forge's face. Then I remember the game in Mallorca. I brought home a little under $2.5 million. Not bad for a night's work.

I shift, not sure if I want to press against him or pull away, and Forge's erection nestles into the crack of my ass. *My naked ass.*

How . . . ? The hand against my stomach stiffens and pulls me closer.

I give in to the devil riding my shoulder and rock backward, pressing harder against him.

"I hope like fuck you're awake and know what the hell

you're doing." His voice is rough from sleep as his hold tightens on me, sending shivers through my body and peaking my nipples.

"And if I wasn't?"

"You'd wake up to an entirely different type of alarm." His cock pulls away and slips through the gap in my thighs. "Fuck, you're already wet."

With a sharp inhale, I bite down on my lip harder to keep from moaning. It feels so damn good. I know I shouldn't tilt my hips just the right angle to nudge the head of his cock against my opening, but I can't help it.

"Fuck, Ace . . ."

"Yes, fuck me. Right now."

I don't know what it is about this moment, but suddenly it feels like this is the most natural thing in the world to wake up with him curled around me, just before his thick shaft tunnels inside me.

I want it. I won't apologize for it. I press down against him, and my breath catches as his girth stretches me wide.

Forge's hands move, one covering my pussy and the other cupping my breast to roll my nipple between his finger and thumb. He groans as he bottoms out, and my head tips back.

His lips find my neck, and he presses a kiss against my skin. "So fucking beautiful," he murmurs before he pulls back.

Each stroke takes me higher and higher, waking up every bit of my body in the most exquisite fashion. This isn't like any of the other times. It's somehow more intimate because we're both moaning and groaning as we destroy each other.

My orgasm builds steadily, helped along by his clever fingers strumming my clit. *It's too much.* I struggle to grab his wrist to pull it away, but his other hand pins me in place. I can't escape from the blinding pleasure—I can only lie there, letting him give me everything I never knew I needed.

When my orgasm finally shatters me, I moan his name. "*Jericho.*"

As soon as the last syllable leaves my lips, it's like I've flipped a switch, turning him into an insatiable beast.

He pulls me tighter against him and locks his arms around me, fucking into me with more force as I hurtle over the edge again. My head whips from side to side as his teeth scrape down my neck and dig into the hollow of my shoulder.

"Jericho!" I scream his name again as I lose every semblance of control.

When I pull free of her body, I realize what I just did. *I didn't wear a condom.*

I've always worn a condom. Always. I never wanted to take a chance of giving someone a hold over me that I couldn't escape. But with Indy, I didn't think twice.

I already married her without a prenup. Why the fuck would I be worried about planting a kid inside her?

I'm not.

The bold reality of it shocks me to my core.

"I'll get you a towel. Hold on," I tell her as I roll out of bed. As soon as I hit the bathroom, I remember what the Russian said just before he left.

"We shall toast to the Federov line being continued, even if it has to be mixed with your American blood."

Is that what I want? I've honestly never considered having kids. They've never been a dot on my plan for what the rest of my life looks like.

Suddenly, the possibility that I could have gotten Indy pregnant changes the picture drastically and permanently. *What if I do want to leave a legacy behind?* There'd be no mother as fierce as Indy. She'd shred anyone who tried to harm her child. *She'd never abandon her child either.*

I stare into the mirror at the man I've become. The black hair I inherited from my mother, too shaggy and in need of a cut that I can't bother to find time for. Dark gray eyes from a father I never knew, eyes that question everything and cut through everyone I meet. A nose that hasn't been broken since the first time Ruben hit me with a closed fist, and it never healed straight.

Beyond the brute staring back at me, I see the kid I was. The one who was willing to risk dying to have a chance at something better. Just like I'm willing to die for Isaac's vengeance.

But the flame of revenge that usually burns so brightly is dimmed right now by the vision of a future I couldn't imagine before this moment.

Can I have both? Or will I have to choose?

I owe Isaac everything for the life I live. That will never be in question.

I shove aside the vivid picture of the future I can't allow myself to think about and tear my gaze away from the mirror. After cleaning myself, I yank a towel off the rack and dampen it with warm water, then stride back to the room and offer it to the woman in my bed.

My wife.

There's also no question that she has changed everything. Is changing me. And I don't know what the fuck I'm going to do about it.

Bright red hints of color appear on Indy's cheeks as soon as I hand the towel to her. "Um, thanks."

She looks away as she cleans up, and I know I should turn to give her privacy, but I don't. I keep my gaze locked on her face.

When she finishes, she wraps the sheet around her,

offering the towel back to me. I take it and continue to watch her in silence.

"I'm going to shower."

"Are you on the pill?" The question comes out of nowhere, and I didn't even know I intended to ask it.

All the color drains from Indy's face. "No. I'm not. Fuck. I didn't even think—"

"It's fine. We'll deal with the outcome, regardless."

Her blue eyes widen. "What the hell does that mean?"

I shrug as if this means nothing to me, when suddenly I've become very attached to the idea of Indy pregnant with my child. Call it a primordial mentality. Call it fucking crazy. It doesn't matter which, because it just *is.*

"We both took part in what just happened, and we'll deal with the consequences together, if there are any."

When her brow furrows, I wish I could see inside her head and know what the fuck she's thinking, because it could change the vision I just saw of what the rest of my life could look like. *The one I just told myself I couldn't think about.* If she snatches that possibility away, I'm left with what now seems like a cold, barren road where the only thing that keeps me going is revenge.

This is all the Russian's fault. He had to get philosophical, and it's rubbing off on me against my will.

"I'm not just going to *deal with the consequences,* Forge. If I'm pregnant, I . . . I'm not just *taking care of it.*"

A rush of relief sweeps through my system. "Good, because that's not what I was suggesting."

The lines of confusion deepen on her forehead. "Wait. What?"

I lean down over her until our noses almost touch. "Don't worry about it until there's something to worry about. Okay?"

"That's easy for you to say." Indy drops her gaze to the sheet fisted in her hand.

"The only reason it's easy is because it's *you*."

Her head jerks up, surprise widening her blue eyes. She studies my face, and I have no idea what she's looking for, but she must find it. "We should be fine, but thank you for not insisting that this would be my problem to deal with if . . ."

"Of course not." I straighten and hold out a hand. "Shower and breakfast?"

A few beats pass before Indy takes it, almost like we're calling a truce. "That would be great. Thank you." Her words are quiet and measured, as if she's not sure how to process the conversation we just had. That makes two of us.

I help her out of bed and she brings the sheet with her, clutching it to her body. If she feels like she needs the armor, she can have it. For now.

"How was the game?" I ask, knowing that if there's one subject to get her talking confidently, that should be it, given the bag I locked in my safe.

Indy's face morphs from caution into something completely different. *Blinding joy.* "I won. I slaughtered them. No one will doubt again that I'm an opponent most men wouldn't dare face."

Her smile is so broad, it sets off little lines around the corners of her mouth and eyes, and I've never seen anything more beautiful in my life.

"There was never a doubt that you're a formidable opponent."

She shrugs, her smile dimming a few watts. "When I played you, I looked like an amateur."

"No." I disagree, shaking my head. "You were anything but that. It just so happened . . . I got lucky that night. Perhaps luckier than I've ever been in my life."

"I want to play you again. I want to redeem myself. Prove to you that I can win against anyone." Her chin lifts as her tone takes on a haughty edge that sends a punch of lust to my dick.

I'll play her again . . .

"For the right stakes, you just might tempt me," I say.

Her gaze dips to my midsection, and I realize she's staring at my cock.

"My eyes are up here, madam."

Indy steps forward, still clutching the sheet, but her smile takes on a teasing edge.

"I think we can come up with stakes that'll tempt you just fine, *Jericho*. But in the meantime . . . I'm ready for breakfast, and I want to count my money."

"*Y*our avarice might even trump my own," Forge says as I dump out the bag of cash on the dining room table, even before all the dishes have been cleared away.

I glance at him, and the easy expression on his face calms the doubt that's plagued me since he pointed out what we'd done—have sex without a condom.

Considering my past, accidental pregnancy has never made my long list of things to worry about. But when Forge sounded like he was suggesting that an abortion would be the right option, I freaked, and my protective instincts over a child that likely wasn't even conceived shot into overdrive. I'd go to war to protect my child, regardless of the circumstances of its conception. When I finally realized that wasn't his intent, the weight lifted from my chest and I could finally breathe easy again.

Like I said, the odds aren't in our favor, but I'm glad I know where we stand on the issue. Even I can't lie to myself and say I don't want to repeat exactly what happened this morning again and again.

I'm dick-struck. That's all.

Either way, I put it out of my mind as much as I can with the shirtless temptation in front of me, and focus on the stacks of banded cash.

I'm riding high on the rush of my win, plus I've had killer multiple orgasms already today, so there's literally nothing that could take the wind from my sails right now.

I pick up a stack of hundreds and hold it up to my nose, inhaling the familiar scent. "I like money. I'm not afraid to say it. Maybe it's gauche, but who the hell cares?" I set it back on the table and grab another to organize them into stacks. "I remember the first big pot I ever won. I didn't even bother to go home. I went straight to Alanna's and dumped it on her kitchen counter, and she burst into tears because she thought I robbed a bank."

Forge's chuckle joins mine. "What did she say?"

"We have to get you out of the country."

"That's true love, right there." Forge flashes a smile, and *oh my God, he has dimples.* Not even fair. "She was willing to smuggle you away to escape prosecution."

I snatch up another bundle and try to erase the dimples from my mind. Easier said than done. I focus on the task ahead of me and keep the conversation light, because my emotions need a break from the whiplash of the last few hours.

"There's nothing she wouldn't do for me or Summer. We're her life, which sometimes seems unfair, but I think that's the way it was meant to be."

"I have no doubt of that," he says, pushing more of the money toward me. "I often wondered why Isaac took me under his wing instead of sending me off to social services after I healed up."

I shoot another look at him. "Healed up?"

Forge's smile disappears. "I had a rough childhood. It wasn't a good time."

"Your parents hit you?" Dread curdles in my stomach at the picture of a small boy with messy black hair and serious gray eyes dodging blows from an adult who should only love him.

"Not my parents. I didn't know my father, and my mother left me with her brother and his wife. My uncle liked to drink and didn't like kids. It wasn't a good combination."

He looks down at the cash in his hands and thumbs through the stack like he's counting it. I can't help but wonder how much it cost the strong and capable man he is now to admit that to me.

"I'm so sorry."

He lifts his head, his expression neutral. "There's no need to be sorry. If not for that, I wouldn't be where I am today."

Even if he can brush it off easily, I can't forget the picture of a battered boy. But he doesn't want my sympathy. I know enough about the man to guess that. Just like I don't want his pity for the things I had to do for Summer and me to survive. I'm proud of how I fought against the odds and won. No one can ever take that away from me, just like no one can take away the blows that forged him into the man he is today.

"Life does somehow seem to work in strange ways, even when we don't understand why." I say the words absently, but my mind latches onto them as soon as they leave my lips. *Was I meant to end up married to this man? If so, why? And for how long?*

While I'm grappling with these questions I can't answer, Forge finishes stacking the money and pushes it toward me.

"I agree, to a certain extent. But if you want something, you have to earn it. Isaac taught me that."

I nod in agreement. "I learned that early. No one in this

world owes you a goddamned thing. At least, not if you grow up without parents like we did."

It's strange to think that's one thing we have in common.

"How long were you on the streets, taking care of Summer alone?" He leans back in the chair and threads his fingers behind his head. His abs and pecs ripple with the movement, and I knock one of my piles over.

Looking down, I scoop it up and try to remember the question he asked. *How long were we on the street?*

"Long enough that it was a blessing to find someone who wanted to help us, even if I didn't trust her."

"I can't imagine you trusting anyone easily."

My gaze lifts to his. I focus on his face, and not how much I want to jump out of my chair and make myself at home on his lap.

Stop it, Indy. Pull it together.

"I slept next to Summer for months, worried that Alanna might turn out to be some kind of creep, even though my every instinct said that she was the real deal."

"I'm glad you found her."

"I'm glad you found Isaac."

For a few moments, we stare at each other, and it feels like a bond snaps into place between us. We have common ground that I never realized. Forge isn't just an arrogant asshole. He's . . . real.

And that makes him even more dangerous to me.

I break our stare and bring my attention back to where it needs to be. *The money.* It's the only thing I can count on for sure.

I do a quick mental tally. "Two point three million. Not too shabby."

"Not too shabby, indeed," Forge says as he releases his grip on his neck and sits straight. "What are you going to do with it?"

I tilt my head to the side like I have to consider what I've already decided. "Spend some. Celebrate a little. Because I like pretty things just as much as the next girl. Invest the rest. Make more money."

With both elbows on the table and his hair falling into his eyes, he nods. "You're a woman after my own heart. You have any investment plans?"

I purse my lips and pretend I'm considering rather than getting stuck on the *woman after my own heart* comment. "Mmm. I don't know yet."

"If you need investment advice, I know a guy," he says with a wolfish grin.

"You?"

He shakes his head. "No. You don't trust me yet. But I have a good friend and business partner who's on the island with his wife for vacation and business. He has a gift for making money that I've never seen before. Sometimes I wonder if he's human, but then you meet his wife and see them together, and you realize he's just a man." Forge drums his fingers on the table. "As a matter of fact, they've invited us to dinner tonight, if you're interested."

I try to hide my surprise. *Forge wants me to meet his friends? Be part of his life and not hidden away?* What does that mean?

Cautiously, I clarify. "You want to take me to dinner and introduce me to your business partner and his wife?"

"Yes, I would. Very much."

"Why?"

"Because I think you'd enjoy a night where you're not constantly trying to figure out what's happening three moves ahead."

I swallow the lump forming in my throat, because I'm not sure how to feel about this at all. Dinner with friends sounds

so normal . . . and not like our marriage is based on something *financially beneficial* to Forge.

Maybe I can learn more about him. Figure out what
makes him tick. *Figure out how to make him want me for me.*

The last thought strikes out of nowhere, but I can't say
that it's a lie.

"Okay. I'll go."

33

FORGE

*J*ndy changes her outfit seven times. I know because I count, and she's officially run out of what she considers proper clothes for drinks by the pool and dinner.

"If you don't make up your mind, I'll have my personal shopper send an entire store of clothes over."

She spins around in the bedroom and shoots me a look that says I would have done better to keep my mouth shut. Something about this whole day feels domestic in a way I've never experienced, and instead of unnerving me, I don't want to lose it.

The scowl on her face says I'm doing just fine.

"I'll figure it out. I just . . . I don't know what to expect. I usually study people before I meet them in real life."

"Stop worrying. You'll be fine. They're good people. If I thought there would be any issue, I would've said no and not brought it up."

She scrunches her nose. "I know I'll be fine. I can handle myself. I sit at the poker tables with billionaires and sheikhs."

"I know you can. Once you figure out what to wear . . ."

Indy shoots me the middle finger. "I'll be ready in an hour."

"Good, because otherwise we'll be late." I take a step toward the door, but Indy tosses a shirt at my head.

With one brow tugging upward, I stop. "Yes?"

"Just so you know, I'm paying for *something* tonight."

Her expression is mulish, but I push back anyway.

"That's not necessary."

"Maybe not to you, but it is to me. I don't care if it's the appetizers or dessert, or even a damn rose for his wife. I'm paying for *something*. I am a millionaire, after all. It might not be much compared to what you have—"

I almost start laughing, because technically, as long as we're married, what's mine is also hers. But clearly, Indy doesn't think that way, which confirms for the dozenth time that she's nothing like any other woman in my past.

"You're a multimillionaire, Ace. Don't sell yourself short. I'll make sure you can spend some money tonight. You have my word."

Her chin juts stubbornly. "Good. Now go. I want you to be wowed when you see me."

With my lips still tugging upward, I step out and close the door. To the empty hallway, I say, "You don't have to worry about that. I always am."

34

INDIA

I'm going to kill him. Literally. With my bare hands. Maybe drown him in the blue waters of the pool beside us. Or maybe drag him out across the beach and let the ocean take him for good.

How could he not tell me that the people we were meeting with were the infamous billionaire Creighton Karas and his megastar wife, Holly Wix?

I keep my forced smile in place through the introductions on the deck of the pool and manage not to choke on my own spit when a woman I've heard on the radio more times than I can possibly count shakes my hand.

"It's such a pleasure to meet you, India. Or can I call you Indy? From what Jericho has said about you, I have a feeling we're going to get along just fine."

For a second, I wonder what the hell Forge said about me, but I'm too tongue-tied to ask.

"The pleasure is all mine, Ms. Wix. Or is it Mrs. Karas? What should I call you?"

The breeze rising off the sea sends her loose dark hair

rippling out behind her like she's in a photo shoot. The woman is even more stunning in person than on TV.

"Call me Holly, and I'll call you Indy. I have a feeling we're going to be good friends."

Holly's Southern twang reminds me that she wasn't always married to a billionaire, but won her first recording contract on a TV show. Now she sells out stadiums all over the world. I would expect her to be dripping with diamonds and wrapped in couture, but she's dressed in a flowing white-and-blue sundress and silver gladiator sandals.

"Holly." I say her name like some kind of idiot and then snap my mouth shut as her husband extends his hand.

"It's a pleasure to meet you, Indy. I'm Creighton. Or Crey, if you prefer. We can be informal since you helped me win a bet with a friend of ours."

"A bet?" I wheeze out the word.

"Forge swore off marriage at one of our meetings, so of course, a friend and I wagered on how long it would be before he took the plunge."

I glance at Forge, whose brows seem to lift in amusement, which is the opposite of what I would expect from him when faced with a friendly jab of that nature.

"I didn't know what the world had in store for me yet." He curves the hand on the small of my back around to settle on my hip. "But you also didn't tell me about the bet. I can't believe Riscoff was willing to take you up on it."

"He was the one who came up with the idea."

Forge's body vibrates with his chuckle. "Of course he was. I'll have to make sure to let him know how happy I was to prove him wrong."

"Your table is ready, Mr. Karas. Would you like me to bring over a bottle of champagne? It would be my pleasure," a server says as he waves toward the private area screened off on three sides with modular bamboo walls, just to the side of the pool.

"I've never turned down champagne, except when I was pregnant," Holly says, her accent growing stronger. "I'm sure not going to turn it down now."

Forge's hand tightens on my hip as we follow the server toward the table. "Champagne is perfect. Indy's ready to celebrate her win last night at a game in Mallorca. Over two million. Kicked every man's ass at the table."

For some reason, hearing Forge brag about me sends a shock wave of surprise through me.

We all settle into our chairs, and Creighton's attention is on me. "Impressive. Although not surprising, considering that your reputation precedes you."

Wait, is he saying he's heard of me? Like beyond what Forge told him?

"You follow poker, Mr. Karas?"

"Creighton." He corrects me, lifting a glass of water to his lips. "And not regularly, but even I remember hearing tales of a woman they called Queen Midas when I spent some time working on a project in Vegas."

Whoa. Not what I expected to hear. But it sets me at ease and makes me feel like I'm not the odd one out at the table.

The server returns with a bottle of champagne, and after Creighton approves it, he pours each of us a glass.

"I didn't play in Vegas long. Too many Americans with chips on their shoulders and something to prove."

Holly bursts into laughter, nearly knocking over the champagne as she reaches for it. "That sounds about right. There's nothing like good old-fashioned arrogance. I imagine you're just as well acquainted with it as I am."

I cut my gaze to Forge over the top of my champagne flute. "I'm getting there."

"You can't put me in the same category as him."

Creighton waves at Forge as he protests to his wife. "He's barely civilized. I couldn't even get him to leave his damn boats and come to land to discuss my first proposal."

"They're ships, not boats, dammit. And what can I say? I prefer the ocean to most people," Forge says with a lazy lift of his chin.

"So, how did you end up in business together?" I ask before taking a sip of champagne.

Creighton snorts and looks at me. "I badgered him. Threatened to land on the deck of his *ship* whether he gave me permission or not. And when he finally said he'd give me an hour of his time, the man barely spoke two words during the meeting."

The server returns, and Forge and Creighton both order whiskey.

"And then what happened?" I ask as soon as the server disappears beyond the bamboo wall.

"I got to the technical part of my proposal, and he proceeded to point out every single assumption I had wrong and explained why I would lose every penny I invested if I stuck to my original strategy, because I didn't know shit about shipping."

I look between the two men, and Forge's posture is more relaxed than I've ever seen before.

"And was he right?" I ask Creighton, already guessing the answer. Forge doesn't strike me as the kind of man to speak on a subject when he's not certain.

"Completely. He didn't even rub my face in it. He just told me how to do it correctly, and we made a shit-ton of money."

"Cheers to that!" Holly lifts her champagne in the air, and the rest of us follow suit.

I like them, I decide. *But I like my husband even more.*

35

FORGE

*I*f there's one thing I'll never have to worry about, it's whether Indy can hold her own in a social situation. She's a brilliant conversationalist, witty, self-deprecating, and just generally fascinating.

She's charmed Holly and Karas. I know it wasn't something she set out to do, but she did it all the same.

Dinner has been cleared away, and we're nursing the remainder of our drinks. I should be thinking about how quickly I can get Indy home and naked, but I don't want to cut this short. She's enjoying it too much to bring the night to a close, even if the sun is setting behind us and the breeze off the Mediterranean cools with each passing hour.

"You find an artist you think has talent, and then you sign them to your label? Just like that?" Indy asks Holly with an awed expression on her face.

"Pretty much. I go with my gut. I can tell who wants it bad enough, and who isn't willing to work hard enough for it."

"I thought it took months and a million committees before a record label would sign someone."

Holly tips the rim of her glass at her husband. "It does, unless your husband decides to go over your head and *buy your record label* for you."

Indy's blue gaze bounces from Holly to Karas. "No way. He didn't."

"Oh, he sure did," Holly says as Karas picks up the bottle and pours the remains into his wife's glass.

"You forgave me eventually. I think you even thanked me."

"Men," Holly says. "What do you do with them?"

Indy finally shifts in her chair to face me. "Don't think I forgot you said you'd let me pay for something tonight. I meant it. And don't go buying the freaking hotel so you can use the argument that it's really already bought and paid for."

With any other woman, I would have said it was the champagne that helped make her comfortable in the situation, but I know that's not it. Indy has a hard-won confidence about herself that comes from the way she had to survive. I recognize it because it's the same way I am.

I haven't been able to stop thinking about what she said earlier. That life seems to work out the way it's meant to.

Part of me wants to start believing what's between us is real and could actually last, but my cynical side won't let me give in to that idea. It's not like buying a record label behind her back; I lured her into marriage without telling her the true reason why. She's only staying for the money. I'd be a fool to think she won't walk away the second the divorce papers are signed and the deposit hits her account.

And that's no one's fault but my own. Pushing the stabbing regret aside, I lift the tumbler of whiskey off the table and down the last sip.

"I promise I won't buy the restaurant or the hotel," I say, and shoot her a wink to cover the morose turn of my thoughts.

"And you're definitely not paying for dinner," Karas says, slapping a hand on the table.

"But—"

"It's already been charged to our room. How about I invest some of your poker winnings, and we can consider this a business dinner that I'll then write off, and you won't feel guilty because you're helping me pay less taxes."

"Like you weren't writing it off already," Holly says with a playful roll of her eyes.

Karas rises and steps behind his wife's chair to pull it out. "Of course, but you didn't need to spill all my secrets."

"Hardly a secret. But now, I think we need to go walk. I want to see this castle that I was told I couldn't leave the island without seeing," Holly says, lifting her chin to look straight up at him. Karas takes the opportunity to lean down and press a kiss to her lips before helping her out of her chair.

Indy's eyes light up. "You haven't seen it yet? It's not far. An easy walk. Let me be your tour guide. And . . . just so you know, there are some incredible ice cream shops on the way."

"I'm sold," Holly says as she stands.

"What do you say?" Indy asks me. "Want to go explore like tourists?"

I pull out her chair and offer her my hand. She slides hers into it, and I squeeze tight.

"Lead on."

36

INDIA

*H*olly is enamored with Castell de Eivissa and its weathered stone walls and their carved inscriptions. As we wander through the medieval structures, I realize how lucky I was that my mother decided to disappear *after* she brought us to this island. It's been my home for so many years, I've started to take its beauty for granted, and I wonder if Jericho has done the same.

Jericho.

His first name is popping into my head with more and more regularity, and each time, I have to check myself. This time, I stumble on the cobblestone street, and his hand is there to steady me.

"You okay? Too much champagne?"

"No. No, I'm fine. Just missed a step." I can't tell him the reason I missed a step is because of him.

After learning about his childhood this morning, and now seeing him with friends while he jokes and laughs at playful ribbing, he's no longer this forbidding titan of industry or ruthless opponent. He's flesh and blood.

I sneak a glance over my shoulder as the sea breeze

ruffles his hair and the dimming light casts shadows from his sharp cheekbones. *Incredible flesh and blood*, I amend, and someone I like spending time with.

Maybe even more than like it. I'm starting to crave his droll comments and sarcastic wit. He makes me smile, and that's not something I thought I'd ever say.

Not to mention, he has the world's most incredible penis and he knows how to use it.

Maybe being Mrs. Jericho Forge isn't the worst thing in the entire world. He's done nothing but help me so far, and while I know there's plenty in it for him, he didn't lie about it. He just didn't tell me the whole truth about his motivations.

In his position, I probably would have done the same thing. He took one hell of a risk when he bet on me, and I'm starting to wonder if losing at La Reina wasn't actually the best thing to happen to me yet.

Only time will tell . . . and I set the clock on that running with my ultimatum that he close his deal and let me go.

The word *divorce* doesn't sound quite so appealing as it did before.

Thankfully, before I can think more about the constantly changing landscape that is my marriage, I spot the ice cream shop that I only go to when I'm truly splurging.

"Are you in the mood for dessert yet?" I ask Holly, pointing across the street.

"Girl, I'm always in the mood for dessert." She pats her sundress in the vicinity of her belly. "Especially when I'm not on tour."

I step out of the circle of Forge's arms and wave my finger between him and Creighton. "I'm buying, gentlemen. Don't even try to stop me."

37

FORGE

$\mathcal{T}$he women are still eating their ice cream when my phone vibrates again.

Fuck. The last thing I want to do is let this night be interrupted by business, so I ignore it. That's when Indy pulls hers from her purse and rises from the small café table.

"Excuse me a moment?" She holds out the phone so I can see the screen. "It's Alanna."

I palm my phone as she steps away and see I've missed two calls from Summer. *Why the hell would Summer be calling me?*

Before I can call her back, Indy tosses her ice cream in the trash and rushes back to the table. "We have to go."

I'm out of my seat before she's done speaking. "What's wrong?"

"The guests in Alanna's efficiency apartment are tearing it apart. She's scared, and the police said they couldn't be there for an hour or more. Summer is threatening to try to stop them herself." Indy grabs at my shirtsleeve to pull me away.

"Sounds like you have somewhere more important to be," Karas says as Holly gasps.

"Yes, go. Please. Take care of it. We'll see you again. I promise."

"It was so nice meeting you both," Indy says with worry lines creasing her brow. "I'm sorry the night has to end like this, but—"

"Go," Karas says. "It's fine."

I grab Indy's hand, and together we rush down the sidewalk in the direction of Alanna's building. A car won't get here more quickly than we can go on foot because of the congested, winding streets. Even a taxi isn't going to be quicker.

Then I look down at her shoes, tall heels that are going to cause her to break a leg if she tries to run.

"I'll carry you," I say, but Indy shakes her head. "This isn't the first time I've had to run in these Manolos, and probably won't be the last. Let's go."

She tugs at my hand. We dart through the cars, and I use my body to shield her from oncoming traffic.

We reach the corner, and one of her heels sticks between the cobblestones. Indy falls forward as she steps right out of it.

I reach for her to steady her before I yank the shoe free and push it into her hands. "Hold this," I say, then lift her into my arms and break into a jog.

"I can run."

"And I can run faster."

Any further protest is silenced as I turn the corner and Alanna's building comes into view. Summer is out front, looking around for God knows what. She spots us immediately.

"Where the hell is your security guy? I thought someone was watching the building?"

I glance around to see the dark sedan parked on the street and wave a hand. Koba jumps out.

Fuck, I should have called him and sent him up first. But my only thought had been to get here as fast as possible.

"What the hell's going on?" he asks at the same time I do.

"I don't know exactly," Summer replies. "I assume they're fucked up and got into a fight. We can hear dishes breaking and furniture cracking. Alanna is losing her mind, and the police are useless."

I lower Indy to her feet and she shoves on her shoe. The four of us rush into the lobby as the elevator is closing, but I shove my arm between the doors. "Did they hurt you or Alanna?"

Summer whips her head from side to side. "No. She knocked, and they yelled through the door. They wouldn't open it. I went over there and pounded until one of them smashed a plate against the door and called me a cunt. Then I phoned the police."

"We'll take care of them." Anticipation pumps in my veins, the same way it did when I ran after the guy who snatched Indy's purse in Saint-Tropez, and then again when I got her back from Bastien. No one fucks with me or mine.

"Which apartment?"

"Six B," both women say in unison.

"Go sit with Alanna," I tell Indy and Summer when the elevator opens to her floor. "Assure her everything will be fine."

I don't wait for my orders to be followed before Koba and I stride toward the apartment. I didn't really need to ask which unit it was because the sound of destruction gets louder as we close in on the door.

Fucking assholes.

I nod at Koba and point to the door. "One. Two. Three."

Together, we kick the white wood and the door flies open, hardware bursting apart from the force.

"What the fuck?" a man yells from inside, but Koba has his gun drawn as he steps across the threshold and I follow.

The voice belongs to a twenty-something kid, not a full-grown man. He goes quiet at the sight of the gun, but his friend sends a broken plate flying like a Frisbee at my head.

I bat it away with my forearm, and it slices across my skin with a sharp sting. "You picked the wrong apartment, mother-fucker." I stalk toward him as he stumbles back against the wall.

The room is a wreck. Broken glass and wrecked furniture everywhere. Even the couch cushions are slashed open. I don't know what the fuck they thought they were doing, but it comes to an end now.

I grab the kid who threw the plate by his collar and lift him up. "What the fuck is wrong with you?"

"Put me down! No one invited you to the party."

That's when I see the two younger women cowering on the other side of the room. *Fucking hell.*

"Are you hurt?" I bark out the question, and they shake their heads.

As I turn my attention back to the punk in front of me, he kicks out with one leg, catching me in the groin, and pain shoots from my gut.

This little fucker is going to be lucky to survive the night.

I toss him onto the floor in a heap as Koba points his pistol at him. "Move, and he just might fucking kill you."

The kid's eyes widen.

I look at the friend who backed down as soon as we entered. He can't hold still. His hands are shaking as he picks at his clothes.

"What the fuck did you take?"

"Meth. I think they took meth," one of the girls says. "We tried to leave, but they won't let us go."

Jesus Christ. These two pieces of shit did all the wrong things.

"You can go, but write down your names and numbers in case the police need statements."

"But—" the girl who spoke starts to protest.

"You want to stay until the cops get here instead?"

They both shake their heads.

Indy speaks from the doorway. "I'll take care of them. Girls, come with me."

I turn around to look at her waving them out of the room. "Make sure the numbers are good before you let them go."

She surveys the wreckage of the room and glares at the two guys. "Of course."

The kid on the floor growls as the women leave the apartment, and the other one starts pleading, nearly in tears.

"Don't kill us. Please, don't kill us. We were just having a good time and doing what he told us to do."

What. The. Fuck?

"What who told you to do?"

Koba and I move in on the kid, and I fully intend to scare the shit out of him to get him to spill everything.

"I don't know him. He showed us the listing. Told us to rent the place and fuck it up a little, and he'd give us cash tomorrow."

Finally not feeling like I'm going to throw up everything I ate for dinner and dessert from the kick in the balls, I crouch next to the destroyed sofa, hovering over him as my brain works overtime. *Who would want to screw shit up for Alanna, on purpose?*

"Tell me everything you know."

Before the cowering punk can start spilling, the other asshole jumps to his feet and makes a run for the door. Koba tackles him, but the kid strikes out with his foot and kicks the gun from Koba's hand. It goes skittering across the floor. The kid jerks like he's going to dive for it, but Koba beats him to it.

But it was all a fucking distraction. As soon as Koba stands up with the gun in hand, the kid is gone.

Fucking hell.

"Follow him!"

Koba bolts for the door and footsteps pound down the hall.

I turn on the friend he left behind. "Now you're really fucked. You're going to tell me the whole fucking story, from the beginning."

38

INDIA

*T*he two girls, Kelsey and Krystal, are a little shaken, but totally fine after they're away from the guys who wouldn't let them leave while they trashed Alanna's place.

I call myself with each of their cell phones and take pictures of their drivers' licenses. Then I ask them each to tell the story of what happened.

"They just asked us if we wanted to party," Krystal says.

It might not be fair of me, but after getting a better look at their tight dresses and hooker heels, I ask a pointed question. "Did they pay you?"

The girls exchange glances as if trying to silently come up with a story.

"Look, I don't care if you're working. That's totally cool. I just want to make sure there wasn't some other reason you hooked up with them tonight—like you knew they were going to trash the place."

Both girls turn to me, and Kelsey replies. "They didn't pay us . . . but someone else did."

"Who?"

She shrugs. "I don't know. I didn't ask for his name. I just took his money."

What the hell? None of this makes sense.

The teapot whistles in the kitchen, and I stand up. "Alanna's making tea. I'll be right back. Please, just don't leave. We really need your help."

"Are we going to get in trouble?" Krystal asks.

From their licenses, both these working girls are only eighteen, and I can't imagine they planned to become prostitutes when they grew up. It makes me sad, because that could have been me if I hadn't learned to play cards to find a way to support myself and Summer.

"You're not in trouble." I pause, not fully considering what I'm about to say, but I don't care. "And if you would prefer not to go back to working for your pimp, I can help you find another job or get you off the island."

Both Kelsey and Krystal's eyes widen.

"Really?" Krystal says, blinking back tears in her brown eyes.

I nod. "Wait here. I'll be right back."

"And I've got some nice hot tea for you, girls," Alanna says, going right into mothering mode, which is exactly what I expected.

I leave the flat and go back to the efficiency unit, intent on telling Forge what I've learned so he can find out who paid the girls. My gut is telling me this whole situation isn't random, but I have no idea why. Immediately, my mind goes to Bastien . . . but it doesn't add up. None of it adds up.

When I peek my head into the trashed apartment, Forge is alone with one of the guys. Koba and the other one are both gone.

"Jericho." I don't know why I say his first name, but it rolls easily off my tongue, and I have to check myself again. *He's Forge.*

His head whips around. "Is everything okay?"

"The girls said these two didn't pay them. Someone else did."

The guy on the floor scuttles farther into the corner like he's terrified of what's coming next.

"I don't know anything, man." His eyes dart from side to side and he shakes with fear. "Alfie was the one who talked to people. I just came along for the ride. He's the one with the connections. He had us staying at some massive pad up in the hills before tonight, and then said we had to come here to fuck the place up to repay our bill for using the other place."

"Why the fuck did you say yes?" my husband asks him.

"Because I ran out of money, and we don't go home for three days. Alfie said we wouldn't have to pay for anything if we did this, and I'd even walk away with cash in hand."

"Where's home?" I ask, even though he's clearly British from his accent.

"London. We're on holiday."

"Whose house were you staying at up in the hills?" Forge asks.

"I don't know. I didn't ask. The guy must have boatloads of money, though."

Forge looks at me, and I know we're thinking the same thing. *Bastien.*

"Was a red Lamborghini there? Someone coming and going?" he asks.

The kid nods until I'm afraid he's going to shake his brain loose from his skull. "Yeah. It was funny because he'd roll up a couple times a day, and each time, he'd only take one suitcase 'cause that's all that would fit in that bitch. Alfie and I joked that he needed an SUV to save himself some time."

Forge steps back and waves at the kid. "Stand up. Give me your wallet."

"I told you, I don't have any more money. A few quid is

all. I can't pay for all this damage. I barely touched nothing. Alfie was going ape-shit. I didn't do the meth. That shit scares me."

"What did you take?" I ask him, because there's no way he's clean and sober right now.

He wipes his nose, and I don't even need him to answer, but he does. "A little coke. Had some Molly for later with the girls."

"Where were you going in the morning?" Forge asks. "Where's your shit?"

The kid points to the corner where two suitcases sit. "We brought it with us, but I don't know where we were going next. I told you, I don't make the plans. I'm just along for the ride."

"Which case is yours?" I ask.

"The blue one."

I walk to the corner and point to the silver one. "This is Alfie's?"

"Yeah." He nods again before wiping his nose.

"Should I open it?" I ask Jericho. "Or should we wait for the police?"

"They'll fuck up the investigation, if they even bother to open one. No point in waiting."

"Okay." I grab an empty pillowcase, crouch down, and carefully turn the suitcase onto its side and locate the zipper —all without leaving my fingerprints on it and hopefully not wiping off Alfie's. Once it's unzipped, I flip it open, revealing brightly colored clothes. *Strange choice for a guy, but—*

My thought cuts off as I zero in on the heat-sealed bags of pills and powder.

"Jesus Christ. There's enough shit in that bag to get Alfie arrested for trafficking and thrown in jail for years if he'd been here when the police arrived."

Forge's head swivels to survey the contents, and he curses

under his breath. He stares down at the guy on the floor. "You weren't planning on being here when the police came, were you?"

"Nah, man, we were going to bolt, but Alfie wanted to break more shit, and then you showed up."

My brain kicks into overdrive. *If they'd bolted before the police arrived, Alanna could have been nailed for this.* Blood pounds in my ears, and I wonder what the hell is going on here.

I flip the suitcase closed, and the luggage tag attached to it flips over . . . *and it has my fucking name on it.*

39

FORGE

"*N*o fucking way." Indy whispers the statement like an oath.

"What?" I bolt to my feet. I want to go to her, but I don't want to let this asshole get away like the one Koba is hopefully dragging back right now.

She stands and points, her hand trembling.

"My name is on this suitcase. My address. Everything." Indy's voice shakes. "If the cops had gotten here before us, they would've arrested me."

"Not fucking possible."

"Oh my God. Wait." She drops to her knees and flips the suitcase open again and grasps a blue piece of fabric. "No. No way . . . This . . . *How*?" Her voice breaks on the last word as she holds up a shirt. I've never seen it before.

"What?"

She shakes the material in her hand. "It's mine. This shirt is *mine.*"

"How the fuck did someone get it?"

"I . . . I don't know."

She pulls out more clothes. Underwear. A swimsuit. With

each item she removes, my need to kill Bastien de Vere hikes up another dozen notches.

"Why would he do this?" Indy whispers, and I can't stay away from her a second longer.

"Don't fucking move," I tell the kid on the floor before I cross the room and pull Indy's shaking form against me. "He's trying to prove he can still get to you, even if you're mine."

Indy's blue eyes widen with disbelief. "This is insanity. He would've gotten me locked up for fucking life. There's no way the cops would believe this wasn't mine. We have to get it out of here. Now. Everything. The police can't come here until we know there's nothing else planted or hidden."

I squeeze her tighter before loosening my grip. "I'll take care of it. Go back to Alanna's. Get the girls out of there."

Indy swallows, and I release her. She pulls the broken door shut behind her as she exits the room, leaving the suitcase with her *fucking clothes* on the bed. It takes everything I have to shove down my anger and not unleash it on this clueless fuck.

With my jaw clenched, I face him. "What's your name, kid?"

"Reggie." His voice shakes like Indy's, which just pisses me off more.

"Last name?"

"Monk."

"And who the fuck is your friend?"

"Alfie . . . Alfred Littleton."

I take a breath, keeping the rage at bay, even though it wants to rise up and crush him now that I know his name.

"Does Alfie's family have connections? Rich friends?"

Reggie's head bobs again. "Alfie's older brother raised him, and he works for a real important guy. Alfie and I came up through school together. He went home with me on holidays because his brother was always working."

"Have you ever heard of the de Vere family?" I ask him.

The kid's eyes go wide. "Yeah, but how did you know that's his brother's boss?"

40

INDIA

*W*hen I get back to Alanna's, the door is shut. From inside, I hear pounding and yelling.

Oh, Jesus fucking Christ.

I shove open the unlocked door and find the kitchen is empty, and my sister is outside, next to Alanna, banging on the glass door that leads out to the terrace.

I rush over to it, unlock it, and yank it open. "What the hell happened?"

"Those little bitches are fucking awful!" Summer fumes, her chest rising and falling.

"It's my fault," Alanna says, patting Summer's shoulder. "One of them asked if they could take tea out on the terrace, and I said yes. I had Summer help me carry it out and when we were both outside, they locked the door and ran."

"Little cunts. I swear, I'm going to check every street corner until I find them and give them a lesson in hospitality."

"Did they steal anything?" I ask, looking around the room. "Plant anything?"

Summer shakes her head. "They didn't have enough time.

My back was only turned for a second when they slid the door shut, and I realized what they were doing. They just wanted to get the fuck out as fast as possible. Fucking bitch-es." My sister bares her teeth like she's gone feral, and Alanna continues stroking her shoulder to calm her down.

"It's my fault," I say. "I thought they were innocent victims."

Alanna comes toward me and pulls me into a hug. "They probably are, darling, but that doesn't mean they lose their sense of self-preservation. Remember how you were?"

"That's why I'm so pissed at myself. I should've known they'd pull something like that. Because I would've too." Some of my anger fades as Alanna squeezes me tighter.

"It's very sweet that you wanted to help them. You have their names and numbers. Maybe someday you still can," she says as she releases me.

"Unless their IDs are fake. Because I sure as shit wouldn't be out walking the street with my own. You wouldn't either, Indy."

My sister has a point. And even though I have their numbers, they'll no doubt block mine.

"I guess you can't help people who don't want to be helped," I say, my tone rueful.

Alanna smiles at me gently. "Yes, you can. You have to wear them down, just like I did with you. Don't write them off quite yet, darling. They didn't hurt us." She pauses and looks around the room. "And I don't think they stole anything. They were just scared kids running back to the only sense of security they have."

My gut twists at the thought of what they went back to. If, by some miracle, I find those girls again . . .

Thoughts of saving the two young girls flee as Forge comes to the doorway, one hand wrapped like a manacle around the arm of the guy who was in the efficiency apartment, and the other dragging the silver suitcase. Quickly, I tell him what happened to the girls, and he nods to the kid.

"Reggie's got twenty quid on him. He's offered it up to help pay for repairs, but I told him to use it to get the fuck off the island." Forge looks to me. "Did you call off the cops?"

Fuck. "Not yet. Summer, can you call them?"

"Why would we want to call them off?" Summer's blond brows dip together as Jericho's expression turns dark.

"Because we're going to handle this ourselves."

I'm thankful he doesn't tell them about the suitcase. Alanna would lose her mind. My sister fumbles for her phone as his dark gray gaze cuts to Alanna.

"When is your next rental?"

"Not until the weekend, but I'll have to cancel now," she says, wringing her hands.

"No cancelations necessary. My staff will take care of it—including removing the damaged furniture and replacing it with new."

Alanna blinks at it him like he's speaking a foreign language. "I can't afford all that, Mr. Forge. I'll have to find something used—"

"I'll handle it. That's what family does."

The warm feeling that blossomed in my chest earlier comes back tenfold.

Alanna's eyes fill with tears. "Thank you so much. You're truly a blessing, sir."

"It's my privilege. Do you need anything else tonight?"

She shakes her head, and he turns to Summer.

"Call off the cops. If they show up, tell them there was a misunderstanding and apologize. Don't let them in the efficiency apartment. Koba will stay there tonight, so he'll be close in case something happens and you need help."

I crane my neck to look out in the hallway beyond Forge. Sure enough, his blond security guy is standing out there, bent over and hauling in breath after breath like he just ran a marathon.

A vein ticks in Jericho's jaw, and it's obvious he's not pleased that Koba came back alone.

He releases his hold on Reggie's arm and pushes him at Koba before holding out his hand to me. "Let's walk Reggie out to the bus on our way to the boat."

41

FORGE

*R*eggie picks up his blue suitcase and bolts as soon as we hit the street, just as I expected he would. Thanks to my text while we were in the hallway, Donnigan was ready for him and is already trailing the kid. Dorsey meets us in front of the building and takes the handle of the silver suitcase from me. Koba heads back inside.

"The others?" I ask her.

"In place or will be shortly, as you requested, sir."

Indy frowns at me, looking as if she has a hundred questions swirling in her brain. "What's happening?"

"Nothing. We're just making sure the building is locked down, and we see everything and everyone coming and going tonight."

"Do you think someone will try to come back tonight?" Indy asks, concern once again lining her forehead.

"I don't know what they plan to do, but there's no question that Alanna and your sister are completely safe." I grip her hand and squeeze.

What I don't tell her is that my security detail isn't only

watching her sister and Alanna. They're also there to watch Koba.

As much as it pains me to distrust one of my own, especially someone whose loyalty I believed was unquestionable, I'm not taking any more chances. Koba was on duty when Indy got slashed and purse-snatched in Saint-Tropez, and when Bastien grabbed Indy off the dock. And now tonight, with him letting that fucker Alfie Littleton, someone with connections to de Vere, get away . . . it's all too convenient, and I don't believe in coincidences.

If I have a traitor within my organization, I will find out and I'll deal with him accordingly. When I'm done, whatever de Vere's paying him won't have been enough, because the price of betrayal will be his life.

"Are you ready to depart, sir?" Dorsey asks, waving to one of the nondescript black sedans I keep on the island.

"Yes, we're ready."

She loads the suitcase into the sedan, and I keep an eye out for cops who might have been conveniently tipped off and ready to strike. I have enough of the department on my payroll that it shouldn't be an issue, but I'm not taking any chances.

I open the back door for Indy and wait until Dorsey closes the trunk to slide inside.

"De Vere is behind this. I don't know what the fuck his angle is right now, but he's changed tactics."

"He was in Mallorca last night," Indy says as Dorsey starts the car, and I wonder why it took her so long to tell me.

"I know. Bates reported in. Belevich was there as well."

She presses back into the seat and sharpens her gaze on me. "I should've figured you already knew. Did they tell you he only approached me once and then backed off?"

I incline my head. "But he watched you all night. They weren't able to identify who he was calling, though."

"Do you think it's possible he set this all up?" she asks as Dorsey drives us to the quay.

"It's possible. De Vere isn't stupid, and if he wanted to cause trouble, this was a good enough plan. Even if it was sloppily executed."

"Did Batman tell you about what Belevich said? That he knew about my sister's kidnapping?"

"Batman?" I ask as Dorsey slows the car at the quay where Goliath waits by the boat.

"Sorry, Bates. Batman is easier to remember, though. He's got that Bruce Wayne aura about him in a suit."

I raise an eyebrow as a blush rises on her cheeks. "Is that right?"

"Anyway, that's not the point. Did he tell you what Belevich said?"

"No, but you should've."

She glances down. "Sorry, I was a bit distracted. I don't know what the hell I was thinking."

Indy quickly runs down everything the Russian told her, and I agree with her—we have to find out where he's getting his information. I have one guess, and I don't want to voice it right now. The last topic I want to discuss is Indy's father. Tomorrow morning, though . . . the man will be hearing from me.

Dorsey opens Indy's door and she climbs out. I push open my own and step out of the car.

"Hey there, high roller. You looking for more company tonight?"

Two women wearing short dresses and sky-high heels stroll toward me.

Indy's breath catches, and I'm sure she's thinking of the two girls who ran from the apartment.

"Sorry, ladies. We're not interested."

The bolder one of the pair struts forward until her hand brushes my arm. "But you look like you'd be a real fun time."

"We're good," Indy says. "Thanks, though."

"You sure?" the girl asks her. "He looks like a lot of man to handle. We can help."

"I'm perfectly capable of handling my *husband*." Indy emphasizes the word as she wraps herself around me, twining her fingers into mine. It's impossible to miss the jealousy in her tone, and I can't deny the satisfaction it gives me.

I squeeze her hand. "I've got all the woman I need right here, ladies. Better luck elsewhere."

They pout but back off. Indy doesn't release me, though. She keeps a tight grip on me as we reach Goliath and the boat.

"I don't share," she says under her breath. "And that includes with women you have to pay for."

I stare down at her face, still gorgeous, even if her lips are pressed into a hard line. "We've covered this ground before, and I was being completely honest. You're everything I need."

42

INDIA

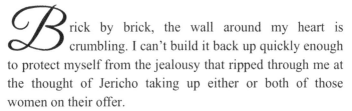

*B*rick by brick, the wall around my heart is crumbling. I can't build it back up quickly enough to protect myself from the jealousy that ripped through me at the thought of Jericho taking up either or both of those women on their offer.

This isn't something I've ever felt before, as irrational as it was. Well, except when it came to Juliette . . .

But the green-eyed monster that clawed its way out of my gut this time was even stronger. *Because I'm feeling things I shouldn't feel.*

I shouldn't care what or who Forge does. But I do care, desperately. And the way he rushed to Alanna's rescue and handled everything . . . If I were capable of swooning in such a situation, I would have.

Which puts me in a very precarious position, watching the walls I've tended so faithfully turn to dust. Once they're gone, there's nothing to protect me from tumbling headfirst in love with this man, which would absolutely be the most idiotic thing I could do, because I already told him I want a divorce.

The salt spray off the ocean should help clear my head as we make our way back to Isla del Cielo, but it doesn't do the trick. When we dock and Forge helps me out of the boat, I'm still a complete mess. I don't know whether I want to pull away or hold on tighter. My instincts are going haywire, and I don't know what the right answer is anymore.

Who would have thought this would be my problem?

I pull my hand free of his as we walk toward the villa, even though I don't want to. *I have to.* I need to put some space between us after this whirlwind of a night so I can sort out how I'm feeling and find some solid ground. My emotions are running too high right now, and I'm not sure I want to face them.

"I'm going to shower and get ready for bed. I'm beat." I toss the words over my shoulder and attempt to make my escape, but Forge snags my hand again.

"What's wrong?" The lines around his eyes deepen as he studies me.

"Nothing," I say, but it sounds like a lie, even to myself. I tug at his hand, but he tightens his grip and forces me to a halt.

"When a woman says nothing is wrong, something is generally very wrong . . . Is this about de Vere and what he did tonight?" My husband's voice takes on a sharper tone when he says Bastien's name.

"What? No. Of course not." At least that much of my answer is honest, because until this moment, I haven't thought about Bastien's next level of attempted betrayal. But now that I am, a tidal wave of emotion swamps me.

Bastien sent people to destroy Alanna's flat. He tried to get me arrested for drug trafficking. He's trying to destroy me because I'm linked to Jericho, and there's nothing I can do about any of it.

"What is it then?" The pale light from the moon glints off

Jericho's messy black hair, and I can't bring myself to meet his eyes. He'll see right through me.

I tug my fingers out of his grip and cover my face with both hands. "I don't know. I need some time and space to figure out what the fuck is going on, because I sure as hell don't know how to process all of this. It's too much. I don't even recognize my life anymore. It's all just too fucking much!"

My voice sounds ragged and tears burn my eyes. *I'm not going to cry in front of him. I'm not going to break down again.*

I take two steps to escape, my lungs heaving as I suck in breath after breath, making my head spin, but Jericho's hands land on either side of my waist and he pulls me back against him, then wraps his hands over my stomach.

"Let me go!" I shove at his hands, even though part of me feels steadier in his arms.

"I won't let you go, Indy. Not like this."

My hands drop lifelessly and I stand still, as if I'm afraid to move because I'll shatter into a hundred pieces like my life has, and I'll never be able to put myself back together again.

Jericho closes his arms tighter around me, pulling my back to his front until the heat radiating off his body warms my skin. With his chin pressing against the top of my head, he speaks in a calming tone.

"I know you've had to shoulder everything yourself for a long time. But you're not alone anymore, and you don't have to hold it all in because you're afraid the people who rely on you can't handle the truth. I'm here, and I'm strong enough to carry every burden weighing you down. If you'd just fucking trust me, you'd know that I've got you. I'm not going to let anything happen to you or your sister or Alanna. I'll keep you all safe. I swear."

He has no idea how seductive those words are to a girl

like me. Someone who has never had someone to lean on without being afraid I might break them too.

I steady my breathing and take two slow, deep breaths.

"That's right. Just breathe."

I want to believe him. I want to let go of all the craziness swirling in my head. All the worries and fears and insane theories. I just want to let it all go for one fucking night.

One heartbeat at a time, I relax into the curve of his body, soaking up his heat and strength. Part of my mind is protesting that I shouldn't get used to this.

"I feel like my life isn't my own anymore," I confess on another ragged breath. "I don't even fucking recognize it. It's like I'm standing on the edge of a cliff, and everything is crumbling beneath me."

Forge's arms wrap around me even tighter. "I'm not going to let you fall. We're going to take this one day at a time, okay?"

One day at a time.

God, that sounds amazing. I could just soak up this moment, let him take my troubles away, and not worry about every little thing that could possibly happen next. If I don't try, I'll drive myself insane.

I take another deep breath and picture myself exhaling all the stress and pressure. With Forge's arms wrapped around me, I feel lighter than I did a moment before. I try it again and again, and with each breath, I pull myself together. My edges are still tattered, but I'm not in danger of shattering right now.

"Thank you. I think I'm good." I straighten, but he doesn't let go.

"I know what you need."

I turn to glance over my shoulder and up at his face. "A hot shower and some sleep?"

"Almost. Come with me."

I lose his arms, and a chill takes their place. I'm not too proud to admit that I don't like it. He takes my hand instead and leads me into the villa and his bedroom.

Instead of stripping or going into the bathroom to turn on the shower, he goes to the far side of the room and pushes the curtain back to reveal floor-to-ceiling glass doors. He slides one open and disappears outside.

A moment later, water splashes into something, and I move toward the noise. "What's that?"

"An outdoor tub. You'll have plenty of privacy. You can soak and just . . . rest."

I follow his voice and peek beyond the billowing curtain to see him leaning over a tub and testing the temperature.

Jericho Forge is running me a bath?

It seems so completely out of character, but then again . . . lately I feel like I don't have a solid grip on this enigma of a man.

"A bath?"

He straightens, and the sound of running water continues. "I'll get you a robe and a towel. It shouldn't be too hot, but you can adjust it."

I track him as he walks by me and back into the master bathroom before I turn around to survey this hidden gem. A small wall wraps around the outdoor lounge space, high enough to give some privacy for the tub, but it still allows a view of the sea beyond from the chairs. A small table sits between them, and on it rests a stubbed-out cigar in a crystal ashtray.

He sits out here at night? I had no idea he knew how to relax. Apparently, there's a lot I still need to learn about Jericho Forge.

He returns with a towel and a robe. "How's the water?"

I shake off my momentary stupor and reach over to put my hand under one of the three faucets. "Perfect."

He nods. "It'll fill quickly. There's a remote for the jets, and even some color-changing lights built in if you want to get crazy."

"I think I'll pass on the lights tonight," I say, and my voice doesn't sound as desperate as it did before. Maybe he's right. Maybe this is exactly what I need.

Forge hangs the robe and towel on a hook and disappears inside again. I check the water level in the tub and decide it's deep enough, then quickly strip off my heels and dress before climbing in. The warm water covers my legs and comes almost up to my belly button already.

Absolute heaven. I close my eyes and lean my head back as it continues to fill.

"I've got some—"

My eyes spring open at the sound of his voice.

Forge's broad shoulders fill the doorway and his white linen shirt hangs completely open, revealing his sculpted chest and the rippling muscles of his torso. Tan linen pants hang off his narrow hips, and I drag my gaze back up to his smoldering one.

My first instinct is to cover myself, but he's already seen every bit of me. Hell, he's touched it all too. *And I want him to touch me again.*

"I didn't realize you were already . . ." He speaks slowly, as if choosing his words carefully before he trails off.

"It's fine," I say, squeezing my thighs together. "What did you have?"

He holds out the bottle. "Bath salts. I've never used them, but I thought you might like them."

The tough-as-nails pirate of a CEO has bath salts in his cabinet . . . and he brought them out for me. I don't know why his thoughtfulness should affect me so much, but it does.

"Thank you. I appreciate it. All of this, actually. And tonight, rushing to Alanna's rescue."

He shakes his head, his dark locks catching on his collar as he steps forward. "It was nothing."

"That's where you're wrong. It wasn't nothing. It was everything. Thank you, Jericho."

"You're welcome," he says, the words clipped as he hands the jar to me. "Do you need anything else before I go?"

One day at a time, I remind myself. *One day at a time.* So, why not end today the way I want and let the chips fall where they may tomorrow?

"Yes."

"What?"

"Will you join me?"

43

FORGE

J can't say no to her. Not when her tanned skin is washed in the glow of moonlight, making her look like a goddess reclining in her bath. And definitely not after I felt her tremble in my arms earlier, and I would have promised her anything to get her to stop.

I meant what I said. I can shoulder her burdens. They're nothing compared to the weight I've carried all these years.

"Are you sure?"

"Please."

Fuck. Hearing that word on her lips kills me. I have to count down from a hundred as I strip off my shirt and pants to try to keep my dick from rising the way it wants to.

While I gave her privacy to undress, she doesn't do the same. No, she watches my every movement.

I've always kept my body strong, toned, and fit so there was no job I couldn't tackle aboard ship, and the discipline and routine it took became part of my life. It was never to get women—because that was never a problem—but now I'm grateful that Indy likes what she sees.

She scoots forward in the water, one arm lifting to cover

her breasts, and I step into the tub behind her. It's big enough for four people, but I've only used it once, when I was nursing bruised ribs from intervening in a fight.

I sit down and lean against the curved back edge. My weight causes the level of the water to rise. Indy scoots back between my spread legs, and like it's the most natural thing in the world, I slide an arm beneath her breasts and pull her closer.

"Lean back. Just rest."

Her stiff posture relaxes as she follows my orders. Together, we watch the stars twinkle in the sky and the moon reflect on the rippling surface of the Mediterranean.

When the tub is full, I turn off the water and reach for the remote to engage the jets.

"Whoa!" Indy bounces up onto my lap as bubbles fill the water.

"I can turn them off."

"No, I just wasn't ready. It's nice. This is all . . . really nice." She leans back against me again, and I thread my fingers through hers.

"I agree."

Several moments of silence pass. I let my mind wander, and of course it goes right to the woman reclined against me. My own frame relaxes in the water, and a feeling of contentment unlike anything I've ever experienced settles over me. This is more than nice. It's . . . a revelation.

This could be my future.

The picture becomes more vivid in my mind. Indy. Me. Building a life together. Hell, if she's pregnant, we could already be heading in that direction. She's never known peace and security like I could give her. I've never given much thought to settling down or having priorities other than my business, but that's changed too. All because of the woman in my arms.

We could make it work . . . if I could ever earn her trust.

She shifts against me, and her spine stiffens as what I assume is a new wave of worries takes over.

"I promise, Summer and Alanna are fine," I tell her. "I won't let anything happen to them. I'll have Goliath go sleep in the hallway from across Alanna's door if it'll help you relax again."

She turns to look over her shoulder, her lips parted. "How did you . . ."

"I'm starting to figure you out. It might take me a while, but I've got a good start."

"Then what am I thinking right now?"

"I honestly don't know, but I know what I'm thinking."

"What's that?" she asks, her brows diving together.

"I want to kiss you so fucking bad, and that's exactly what I'm going to do."

*I*t was ridiculous, but the thought of kissing Jericho Forge right now feels even more intimate than sex. Maybe because I don't have a lot of experience kissing men, and he's only kissed me a few times.

There was a reason Julia Roberts didn't allow kissing in *Pretty Woman*. I may not have understood it before, but I get it now.

Forge brings our joined hands up to my cheek and uses my own fingers to turn my chin toward him. Moving ever so slowly, as if waiting for me to bolt, he lowers his lips to mine.

The remains of the worry and fear that clung to me disappear as soon as my lips part and his tongue sweeps inside.

My hand slides out of his grip as I turn my body around in the tub so we're chest to chest, never losing his mouth. His tongue tangles with mine, and I curve my fingers around the base of his neck, half floating, half resting on top of him.

It's as if I'm suspended in an alternate reality where I'm falling in love with this man who would kick down doors and do whatever it takes to keep my family safe. The kiss goes deeper, and my senses are overwhelmed with wanting him.

The moment is so perfect, I never want it to end, because it's one that may never be able to be replicated.

I pull myself closer to him, planting my knees on either side of his hips and my nipples pressing against his pecs as the bubbling water splashes us both. *I want more.*

His hand slides into my hair, gripping the back of my head like he can't get me close enough. His other arm wraps around my back, pinning me against him.

"I love the way you taste," he says against my mouth, and I moan in response.

Whatever his plan might have been, I know exactly what mine is now, especially with his cock thick and hard between us. I reach down to wrap a hand around it and squeeze.

"Fuck . . . Do that again."

I haven't had enough sexual experience before to know that being told what to do in bed amplifies the experience for me, or maybe that's just the case with Forge. Regardless, I stroke him, working his cock in my tight fist, and my pussy grows wetter and wetter with each tug.

I pull my lips away from his. "I want . . . I want to ride you."

Forge's dark gaze zeroes in on my face as he reaches down to wrap both palms around my hips and lifts me up, a clear *hell yes* response to my statement.

As he lowers me, his lips curve into a heartfelt smile that warms his eyes and eases the harsh lines of his face. I already know Forge is strong, but this man, the one holding me with such care, is gentle in a way that demolishes any remaining barriers I've been reinforcing.

But as soon as the head of his cock connects with my entrance, he stiffens, and I lose the smile I wanted to see on his face forever.

"Fuck, Ace. No condom."

It's stupid and reckless, but I shake my head. "You can pull out. It'll be fine."

It's a horrible plan to count on for reliability, but it's worked its way into my head that if I don't have him right here, right now, I'm going to lose my only chance at something I never knew I wanted. No, something I need. *Him.*

It should be a terrifying realization, but right now, I don't care.

I push the thought of all consequences aside, and for the space of three breaths, my gaze locks on his. I wish I could read the thoughts behind those stormy gray eyes, but I can't. Not yet.

Finally, he lowers me again. He slides me down the hard ridge of his cock, and I bite my lip to keep from moaning out loud as he stretches me wide.

From behind clenched teeth, he grits out, "That feels too fucking good. Jesus Christ. You're going to destroy me, woman."

Not more than you're going to destroy me, I think. *Because I'm not holding anything back now.*

I rock my hips, impatient to move. Forge's grip tightens around my waist, and he leans forward to brush his lips across my jaw.

"Ride me."

FORGE

*I*ndy's pussy is already tight as fuck, but when I tell her to ride me, her inner muscles clamp tight. How the fuck is she so goddamned perfect for me? Right down to the part where she gets turned on when I take control?

With my help, she rises on her knees, letting the warm water lap against my dick, before dropping to take me balls deep. It's the most incredible torture I've ever felt. Slow and steady, she fucks me as the water splashes around us.

I'm surrounded by everything India, and I fucking love it. Maybe too much.

I shouldn't be taking her without a condom. We both know the risks. But maybe some small part of me is hoping if she gets pregnant, then I can keep her beyond the terms of the deal.

Either way, if she wanted me as badly as I wanted her, bare inside her, with nothing between us, I would never say no. My instincts roar with raw, primal need, declaring that this is the way it was always meant to be.

Piece by piece, I've started to figure her out, and the intricate and fascinating puzzle that is my wife is coming into focus. I still don't know what she wants from me, if anything.

Would she ever consider changing the terms of the deal and bargaining away her thirty-day deadline? Could I negotiate my way into her giving me a chance to make this real? It doesn't matter if it's thirty, three hundred, or three thousand days—no finite amount of time will satisfy me. I want more from her.

With that realization firmly in place, I grip her hips and torture myself with her slow, steady strokes. She whimpers, and I lift her up and off my cock.

"You need more to come. Turn around and grab the edge of the tub. I'll give you exactly what you need."

She rises on unsteady legs, and I circle her waist to hold her ass right in front of my face.

I press a kiss to one cheek and then the other. "Every part of you is so fucking beautiful. Someday, I'm going to take that tight little ass and make you come harder than you ever have before."

She shivers, and I release her so she can reach for the edge of the tub as I stand. Her tits hang in front of her, and I cover her back with my chest so I can reach around and play with her nipples.

"Please . . ."

The plea blasts into me, and I can't wait any longer. No more teasing. I need to be buried inside her again.

"Hold on tight."

With one hand, I grab my cock and center it on her entrance. As soon as I get a kiss of the heat of her pussy, I slam inside. Indy moans as her muscles squeeze my dick even harder.

"Oh my God," she whispers. "More. I need—"

My fingers splay over her pussy. "I know what you need."

I pull back and tunnel inside, over and over as I strum her

clit. Water splashes everywhere, and I don't give a single fuck about the mess we're making. All I care about is every whimper and plea coming from her lips.

She's fucking amazing as she pushes back against my strokes, taking me deeper and harder. Her inner walls flutter and then lock down on my dick, trying to hold me captive as she comes.

I take her faster, increasing my pace, stretching out her orgasm as mine threatens to shoot down my spine like lightning and erupts from my balls.

I'm not ready for this to end. I keep fucking her over and over until unintelligible sounds come from her mouth and she comes again.

Only then do I pull out and grip my cock as rope after rope of my cum covers her ass.

I stagger backward, my knees weak, and drop into the water once more. My heart thunders like I swam from here to the shores of Ibiza. Indy's legs wobble, and I reach out to steady her and guide her back down into the water against me.

"I got you."

I press a palm over her chest, and her heart pounds as hard as mine. When the beats slow into a normal rhythm, she releases a long breath.

"I guess you really did know what I needed." She turns her head to look at me over her shoulder like she did earlier, and this time, there's a lazy, satisfied expression on her face. "Thank you."

When she leans toward me and presses a kiss to my lips, I know that there's absolutely nothing I wouldn't do to keep this woman in my life.

My phone chimes in my purse on the nightstand, and I roll over. The first thing I notice is that there's no solid mass of body heat beside me. Despite the twinging soreness between my legs reminding me of last night, I miss his presence.

Yesterday morning started out with exactly the right kind of *bang*, and I wouldn't mind repeating it.

Regardless, it doesn't matter because Jericho is gone.

I sit up in bed and reach for my black Valentino clutch on the nightstand. Instead of seeing a text from Summer or Alanna, like I expected, there's one from an unknown number. The calm I woke up feeling drains away like the water in the bathtub as I unlock the phone to read it.

Your invitation is official. I'll see you in Prague. I'll bring my five million.

MY FIRST THOUGHT is *How the hell did Belevich get my*

number? It's quickly followed by the second question in my brain . . . *Do I really want to go?*

After everything that's happened, I know it's a risk. But pieces of the puzzle are still missing, and no one is going to bring them to me. I have to go find them.

Then there's my reputation . . . Belevich got me an invite to the grand prix, and if I don't show, how will it reflect on me? I know I could make excuses, but after he went to the trouble of securing the invite, it could be argued that I was too intimidated to appear. Poker is still very much a boys' club, and there's a part of my ego that wants to show them that I'm still the better player.

It is my job, *after all.* If I stop playing poker, I would have to find something else to do, and I've never had the temperament for coaching online wannabe players.

It's not just about the money. I can't live without a purpose and a goal. Poker has kept me focused and sharp. It's also a skill that only stays honed to this level if constantly practiced. The grand prix is the perfect way to prove to the world that not only am I the best female poker player, but there's no man I can't beat either.

So, basically . . . I have to go. For myself, and to discover whatever information Belevich is holding back. I would be an idiot not to take this calculated risk.

My decision made, I tap out a reply.

I'LL SEE YOU THERE. Better bring more than five million.

I CLIMB out of bed and spot my robe laid across a chair near the sliding glass doors. I grab it and shove my arms in the long sleeves before peeking beyond the curtain to see the tub. In the morning light, it seems no less decadent. *It is definitely one experience I need to be put on my repeat list.*

With a spring in my step, I head out of the bedroom to find my husband. I check the kitchen first—no sign of him. Not outside on the patio eating breakfast either.

Where the hell did he go?

His office. I make my way back down the hall and knock. Within seconds, I get a reply.

"Enter."

Inside, Forge is seated behind the massive desk and sunlight streaming in through the open curtains. He looks up, and the first thing I notice is that his hair is a mess, like he's been running his fingers through it over and over.

"Is something wrong?" I ask.

"Did you need something?" His habit of answering a question with a question is alive and well this morning.

"Just wondering where you were. Did you eat breakfast?"

"No. I had business to handle." His tone is curt and his posture rigid.

I step closer to the desk, which is covered in files and papers. "What's wrong?"

The dark gray of his eyes looks like the cloud wall of a hurricane. Almost black and completely foreboding.

"Why would you think something's wrong?"

"Because you won't answer my question. You're evading."

His defensiveness tightens my throat, making me feel like I'm standing in front of a stranger, and not the man who promised he could carry my burdens last night.

Forge crosses his arms over his chest and stares at me like there's nothing he'd rather do than hustle me out of his office. Something inside me that was just beginning to bloom wilts.

"There will always be things I can't tell you, India."

Shrinking back, I mimic his posture, crossing my arms over my chest. But in my case, it's a protective gesture.

"I'm not asking for the keys to the kingdom. You looked upset. I was being a decent human being and asking if everything was okay. Don't worry, I won't make that mistake again."

FORGE

*T*he message I got first thing this morning from my helicopter mechanic wasn't one I ever want to receive.

THE CHOPPER'S BEEN FIXED, but we need to talk. There's no way this happened by accident.

I'VE SPENT the last hour in my office racking my brain to figure out how the fuck someone could have tampered with my helicopter.

I already have my suspicions about Koba, and he could have had access to it, but I'm not going to condemn him without proof. Especially because there's no security footage of him near the helicopter while it was on the island.

After questioning the pilot, I still don't have any more answers, except that he only left the chopper unattended for about ten minutes after landing in Mallorca so he could use the toilet.

Which makes me think that I wasn't the target—Indy was.

My instincts say that no way in hell did Federov take care of the threat that caused Summer to get kidnapped, and I'm also not convinced de Vere is working alone. He has nothing to gain from hurting her except knowing it would be a strike at me. Although . . . given my *death by a thousand cuts* plan that I've unleashed over the last ten years, maybe that's exactly what he would do.

Either way, I don't have any final answers to the questions plaguing me, and I need them right the fuck now. Or rather before now, because Indy is looking at me with hurt in her eyes, and I hate it.

Twelve hours ago, she was close to breaking, and the last thing I want to do this morning is drop one more burden on her. But I also can't keep something like this from her.

"The malfunction that kept you from flying back from Mallorca wasn't a routine mechanical issue."

Her eyes widen. "What do you mean?"

"Someone did it on purpose. There's no way it was an accident or routine failure."

Indy jerks back as if someone pushed her. "Someone . . . someone wanted us to crash?"

"Possibly. Or they wanted you to stay put and not be able to leave. But we always have a plan B, and when your gut said something was wrong, you were right."

She uncrosses her arms. Slowly, she walks toward the wooden armchair opposite my desk and lowers herself into it. "Bastien."

"Possibly, but he was there before and during the entire game, so I don't know when he'd personally have had the opportunity. But someone working for him could have done it."

"That motherfucker." Her chest heaves, widening the

gaping lapels of her robe as anger rises on her face. "What is his fucking problem?"

"That's what I'm trying to figure out—whether this goes beyond the revenge I've been exacting, or if this is spurred by something different."

"Like what?"

I tap the contract on my desk that her father marked up while she was away that night. "I know you don't want to hear about this."

She follows my line of sight. "This has to do with my father, doesn't it?"

"Possibly."

She closes her eyes and presses her lips together. "Then just tell me."

"He's a wealthy man. A *very* wealthy man."

"So what?" India asks as the clouds cover the morning sun and the room turns dark.

"That makes you a very wealthy heiress, because you stand to inherit it all."

48

INDIA

I'm nobody's fool . . . except, apparently, when it comes to Jericho Forge. "That's why you married me without a prenup. So you'd get half of everything he has when he dies."

It's not a question; it's a statement. There's no way in hell he would have done such a thing unless it was *financially beneficial.* I hate those words even more now than I did before.

"It crossed my mind, but I also knew there was a very small probability our marriage would last that long." He says it casually, but it feels like a slap to the face.

"If that wasn't your motivation, then why the hell did you marry me?"

"Whether you believe me or not, it wasn't all about leverage. It was also to protect you."

Forge's posture exudes confidence, like he knows he did the right thing and doesn't feel the least bit of guilt over keeping any of this from me.

He tried to tell you, the whisper in my head chimes in. *You didn't want to hear it.* I tell that voice to shut the hell up and glare at the man in front of me, hoping my blue eyes freeze him in place.

"Protect me from what?"

"Whatever you think of me, I wasn't about to find you for your father and turn you over to him without any concern for your safety. I might be a fucking asshole, but even I wouldn't take that chance with someone's life."

Blood thunders through my head like a freight train. "You thought he might want to do me harm after looking for me all these years? And you still told him you found me?"

A muscle ticks in Forge's jaw. *I hit a nerve with that question.*

"I didn't know what his plan was, but I wasn't going to sacrifice you to feed my own ambition. It was my contingency plan. As long as you're tied to me, you're safe."

A choked laugh gets caught in my throat. "Are you serious? Clearly, I'm not fucking safe, because someone messed with your goddamned helicopter and I could've died!"

I shove out of the chair and pace the room. There's too much information swirling in my head now that I never wanted to know.

I buried my head in the sand the last time he tried to tell me about my father, and I shouldn't have. Or maybe I wish I could go back to when I was lying in bed and knew none of this. Either way, I prefer ignorance to the cold, hard truth.

What if my father is a terrible person? What if he's done horrible things? Is that why Forge felt the need to take extra precautions?

Forge's chair scrapes across the tile floor. "I'm not going to let anything happen to you. If you believe nothing else I say, believe that."

I spin to face him. "I don't know what the fuck to believe anymore. All I know is that the sooner you finish this fucking business deal, the sooner I can have my divorce and get back to living my life."

"It's not that simple. Now you know who you are. Other people know who you are. Your life will never be the same as it was before." He stands like a tyrant behind his desk, and I don't like being dictated to.

I jam my hands in my messy hair and grip my head as I pace in the other direction. "And whose fault is that? What did I do to deserve this? I can't control a goddamned bit of it, so why should I have to roll over and accept being a pawn in your fucking game?"

When I spin around again, I drop my hands and use them to punctuate every single last word I have to say.

"No. Fuck that. I'm going to pack my shit and go to Prague and win a boatload of fucking money at the grand prix, and then I'm gone. You'll never find me, Alanna, or Summer ever fucking again."

49

FORGE

*W*hen she says she's going to disappear and never be found, it's like being stabbed in the chest.

I knew I was going to lose her. I knew that from the beginning. But now, facing the reality of it, I can't let that happen.

I shove my hands in my pockets and try to rein in my temper. I fail miserably.

"What the fuck are you talking about? You're not going anywhere. Much less Prague to play some fucking grand prix."

She stalks toward me looking like a warrior princess prepared to do battle with her bare hands. "Don't think for one second that you can stop me. This isn't fucking Alcatraz. You're not my warden. I'm leaving, and I'm never coming back."

A million emotions burst through me like flickering flames, but I smother them all with ice—except the rage. That, I grip with both hands and let fly.

"Try to leave. I. Fucking. Dare. You." I spit out each word like a curse and round the desk to tower over her.

I will fucking intimidate her into following orders if I have to. I won't fuck around with her safety.

The rage turns icy as I consider one last threat. My tone drops low and quiet, just to make sure she understands. "If you ask Bastien to come save you, I swear to Christ, I will kill him with my bare fucking hands."

Indy's mouth drops open and her blue eyes widen with shock. "You think I asked him to come here last time? Don't you get it? I hate him! He's the last person I'd ask for help." She says it so convincingly, but history doesn't lie.

My temper jumps its chain.

"You sure as fuck didn't waste any time running to him for help before. *Right after you took my check for a million dollars on the promise that you would never go near him again.*"

Indy's nostrils flare, and she gives me a mutinous look. "I didn't have a choice! And I didn't care about you then."

Her admission, almost certainly unintentional, stops me cold.

"What did you say?"

Indy's lips clamp together and she backs away, but she can't take back what she said. I fucking heard it.

She didn't care about me then. Which means . . . *she does now.*

"What did you say?" I repeat my question and she shakes her head, sending loose waves of blond hair swinging over her shoulder.

"It doesn't matter. We made a bargain. You close your deal and you give me my goddamned divorce. Until then, I don't want to see you or speak to you if you're going to treat me like a child at best or a prisoner at worst."

She spins on bare feet and races out of my office, a sob breaking from her lips before she slams the door behind her.

"Fuck!" I grab the chair she was sitting in and launch it across the room. The wood cracks when it hits the wall, splintering apart and leaving a mark.

Footsteps come pounding down the hallway, and someone hammers on my office door.

"Sir, is everything okay?" It's Dorsey.

Instead of grabbing the other chair like I want, I stride to the door and yank it open. With my hands clenched into fists and my lungs heaving, I bite out an order.

"Tell everyone that my wife doesn't leave this fucking island, and if she does, you're all fucking fired. Every single one of you. Understood?"

Dorsey stumbles back a step as she nods. "Yes, sir. Understood, sir."

I slam my office door hard enough to crack the wood, then grab the back of my neck with both hands before letting out an enraged roar.

*M*y duffel bag is packed with what little stuff my sister brought, and I'm dressed and ready to get the fuck off this godforsaken rock.

I don't care what Forge says; he can't keep me here. I will steal a boat or stow away or do whatever I have to do. Hell, if I get desperate enough, I'll steal a dry bag and a life vest and dog-paddle myself to shore.

I'm going through my mental list of who I could call that owns a boat when my phone rings in the pocket of my robe. I whip it out and stare down at the screen.

Summer.

"Please tell me there's no more bad news," I say in lieu of a greeting.

"Whoa. You sound pissed. On the rag?"

I roll my eyes at her predictable response to me being upset. "No, but I need a fucking rescue from this island. Forge told me I'm not allowed to leave."

Summer chuckles, and I want to shake her for not taking me seriously. "Why won't he let you leave?"

"He's concerned for my safety," I tell her as I grab a stray pair of panties hanging out of a drawer.

"Well, that sounds kind of sweet."

"Don't even try to take his side. I'll hang up so quick, you won't have a chance to say a single word. Which one of your friends has a boat? Can you call in a favor?" My tone sharpens, and my sister's changes accordingly.

"Okay, okay. We need a boat to come get you. Got it."

Then I remember I didn't call Summer. She called me. "Why did you call? Is something wrong?"

"Not exactly *wrong* . . ."

I wait for her to elaborate, not in the mood to play twenty questions.

"I just wanted to tell you that they've already cleared out all the broken stuff, and cleaners are tidying up everything as we speak. I was going to ask you to thank your husband for Alanna . . . but it sounds like you'd rather stab him."

A teeny-tiny sliver of my rage fades away, but only because I'm not an ungrateful bitch.

"Is that all?"

"Alanna thought she saw one of the prostitutes this morning while she was at the market. I told her that there was no way, but she swears it was one of them. Of course, you know she now probably wants to save them too."

Which was my first thought when I saw them last night. Then I remember what Forge said about my safety, and immediately I extrapolate it to my sister and Alanna.

"Did she have security with her? One of Forge's people?" I chew on my lip, waiting for a response, because I can't stand the thought of Alanna taking chances with her safety if there's some kind of threat now that my identity has been exposed.

"Yeah, he insisted. It annoyed her a little, but she went along with it."

"Good, that's good," I say, nodding even though she can't

see it. "Please tell her that she needs to keep going along with it." *For as long as this lasts,* I add to myself.

"Oh, and Juliette pushed my start date for work back to today instead of Monday. Apparently, she had business in Saint-Tropez that took more time than she thought, so I'm leaving in a few minutes. Wish me luck?"

The last thing I want to think about right now is Forge's ex-mistress, but still, *not an ungrateful bitch.*

"Of course. Be polite and professional. You know you're capable of anything she puts in front of you. And if she tries to test you because of me—"

"Stop." Summer interrupts my rant before it starts. "Don't worry, Indy. I got this. I'll call you tonight and fill you in on all the details."

When my sister hangs up, I realize that there's no boat coming for me. Summer has more important things to do— like secure her future by making a good impression on her new boss.

The whore.

Juliette, not my sister.

Either way, there's no help or rescue coming from that direction. Which means, as usual, I'm on my own.

I open the sliding door that leads from the master suite to the patio and the pool, and the first thing I see is the distinct black boat, the one that looks more like a military attack vessel than a civilian runabout, speeding away from the island. It's still close enough that I can also make out the wind-blown mane of black hair belonging to the man at the helm.

Forge.

Oh no, he didn't. Except, *he fucking did.*

Even more determined to find a way off this island, I yank out my phone and scroll through my contacts. I will not be here when he gets back.

"*I* didn't expect to see you before we left tomorrow. I thought you said you had everything handled?" Creighton Karas asks me as he opens the door to his suite.

I look around the room for Holly, not sure I want to have this conversation in front of her.

"Where's your wife?" I ask Karas as he closes the door behind me.

"A designer flew in from Milan to bring her an entire season's worth of dresses to choose from for her awards-show circuit. They're in the bedroom." He gives me a wry look with his eyebrows raised. "Now, tell me you didn't come here just to see my wife before I gut punch you."

"Trust me, that's the last thing I fucking need this morning."

Karas frowns at my strained words. "What's going on?"

"Federov sent me an email this morning stating that he'd give on everything he marked up, but only on one condition. And there's no way I can agree to that condition without both you and Riscoff signing off on it."

"He's willing to give on all the revisions he made in person?" Karas's eyebrow rises.

If I were in his position, I'd be asking the exact same thing. When someone who has a reputation of being an impossible negotiator says they'll give in on everything, you can't help but wonder why he'd make such an insane shift in behavior.

"In exchange for what?" Karas asks.

"Something you won't fucking believe."

I hold a printout of the attachment to the email Federov sent me with his "must be accepted word for word" addendum to the deal. Without it, he won't agree.

Karas reads over it and looks up at me, just as surprised as I was when I read it. "He's fucking serious?"

"Absolutely."

"But it doesn't make sense," Karas says, rereading the language that states that the only way Federov will consent to signing the contract is if he's made a full partner in the entity Karas, Riscoff, and I created, and upon his death, his daughter will receive his share and all rights related to it.

"It does, when you consider that he doesn't trust me because I married his daughter behind his back."

And I refuse to feel fucking guilty for it. It was the right choice. I'd do it again. Even as I tell myself that, a shred of doubt assails me and I force it down. *I did what I had to do.*

Karas hands the addendum back to me. "Well, hell. This changes things." He walks toward the floor-to-ceiling windows that lead to the terrace. "So essentially, if we agree, you get two shares of the partnership."

A strangled laugh catches in my throat. "Not at all."

Karas turns around, and his sharp stare cuts to my face. "What do you mean?"

"I mean that there's no way in hell my marriage is going to last beyond the moment we sign this deal with Federov.

Indy will divorce my ass before the ink is dry and run as far away from me as possible."

"What the fuck did you do? She seemed fine yesterday."

I jam my hands in my pockets. "You assume it was me?"

Karas's head tilts back and his entire body shakes with laughter. "Of course it was you. That's what men do—fuck up because we can't get our heads out of our asses, especially men who have more money than God and don't take orders from anyone."

I look out the window as well, not sure how to reply. I decide to go with the truth. "She's looking for a boat to get off the island as we speak. I had to threaten to fire all my employees if she manages to escape."

"Jesus Christ, Forge. Don't you know anything about women?"

My hands flex into fists. "Apparently not. I don't expect you to understand the situation."

Karas crosses the room and stops in front of the sideboard. "Come on, you need a drink. I'm going to tell you a story, because you couldn't be more wrong."

Once he's poured us each three fingers of whiskey, we take a seat on the balcony.

"I coerced Holly into marrying me. It might not have been the same situation you're in, but I did it for my own selfish reasons. Mostly because I saw her once and knew I had to have her."

His words sound too familiar, so I stay quiet and let him continue, interested to see where this conversation is going. Mostly because I'm hoping he'll have the wisdom that'll act as my silver bullet to fix what I've clearly fucked up.

"She was in a bad spot," Karas says with his glass dangling from his fingers. "Her record label was trying to force her into a fake engagement with a has-been artist to buoy his reputation. He obviously didn't get the chance to pop the fake fucking question, because I intervened."

"You saved her."

Karas turns to meet my gaze. "In some ways. But mostly, she saved me."

"What do you mean?"

"You know what it's like to have everything. More money than you can spend in ten lifetimes. Never have to worry about the cost of anything when you decide you want it. Having everyone around you kissing your ass and begging for favors. It gets old."

He speaks the truth, but then again, why wouldn't he? He's been a self-made billionaire for longer than I have. My wealth was partly inherited and then grown under the careful cultivation of my rage and plan for revenge.

"A-fucking-men," I say, lifting my whiskey in salute.

"And you also know what it's like to meet a woman who ends the boring monotony of having everything handed to you at your beck and call, or even before you can think to want it. I saw the way you looked at Indy when she'd say something witty or clever. You looked impressed. Proud, even." Karas takes a sip, his expression thoughtful now that he's getting uncomfortably personal.

"What's your point?" I ask as my fingers close tightly enough around the glass in my hand to nearly crack it.

"My point is, when you find a woman who gives you a reason to wake up in the morning that's more than just making more money you'll never be able to spend—you fucking hold on to her with both hands."

"I already fucked that up. She can't get away from me fast enough."

Karas leans back in his chair and kicks his feet up on an ottoman before shooting me a sideways glance.

"If you think I didn't fuck up and drive Holly away, you

clearly give me way too much credit. I did it, and I did it in true self-absorbed billionaire fashion. I put her at the bottom of my priority list. Took for granted that she'd always be waiting until it was convenient for me. And you know what happened?"

"What?"

"I fucking lost her." He takes another sip as I try to piece together his story.

Considering how Karas and his wife are together, there's no way I would ever think he fucked up badly enough to lose her. It seems impossible.

"But you got her back . . ."

Karas sits straighter and a wry grin stretches over his face. "Of course. I'm not a fucking idiot."

"How?"

"I tracked her down and begged her to forgive me for being such a fucking moron, and I made her dreams and goals and wishes the center of my world. I made *her* the center of my world. If you told me the sun doesn't rise and set over the curves of my wife's perfect ass, I'd call you a goddamned liar. It doesn't matter what anyone says or does, or what business deal is on the table. It all comes second to her."

I hear what he's saying, but it seems completely at odds with the man I've come to know.

"You're telling me I should give up this deal with Federov to prove something?"

Karas chuckles over the rim of his glass. "Hopefully it doesn't come to that, but if she's going to walk away, it's not because of this deal. It's because you haven't stopped to figure out what matters to her. You haven't listened to what she says she needs to be happy."

"You know you sound like a sappy self-help book, right?" I lower my empty glass to the table between us and sit forward.

"Fuck off, Forge. I know what I'm talking about. Only one of us is happily married and has the most gorgeous daughter in the world who will never date until I'm dead and buried, because no man will ever be good enough for my Rose."

Karas's entire expression softens when he talks about his daughter, and I can't help but think about the fact that Indy and I didn't use protection. Before her, I never thought I'd be interested in having kids because of my shitty childhood, but now I can see Indy with a little girl, teaching her to bluff at poker. Or me with a little boy, helping him learn to fish off the pier on the island.

Suddenly, I'm jealous as fuck of what Karas has with his wife and daughter. *His family.*

Isaac told me I was his family, and family always came first. *How did I forget something so basic and important? How did I fuck this up so badly?*

I have to fix it. I have no choice. I can't let her go like this.

"What do I do? How do I salvage this thing?"

"First off," Karas says, rising to walk inside the penthouse. "It's not a thing. It's your marriage. And congratulations, it's now your top fucking priority. It takes more work than anything you've ever done before in your life, including building a shipping empire from almost nothing to biggest in the world."

"You're really doing a great job selling this, by the way."

He disappears inside and returns a moment later with the bottle of whiskey. Using it to gesture, he says, "Shut the fuck up, Forge, and listen. Don't, for a single minute, think she's going to be easier to negotiate with than her pissed-off Russian father. That's your first mistake. I don't know what the hell happened between you two, but I do know that you've probably hurt her somehow, and now you have to fix it. What does she want more than anything, right now?"

The argument Indy and I had right before I left storms into my mind. "A divorce."

Karas waves me off as he splashes two fingers into my empty tumbler. "Other than that."

"To play a grand prix in Prague, which is too fucking dangerous to consider after the shit that's gone down."

He narrows his gaze on me. "Are you, or are you not, a fucking billionaire? You could buy the fucking Secret Service to keep her safe, so that's a cop-out. If she wants to go to this thing, and it's that important, you move heaven and fucking earth to give her that."

My jaw tight, I nod. "Go on."

Karas exhales a long breath as he fills his own glass. "You might be a lost cause, brother. I hate to say it, but I don't think there's a romantic bone in your body."

He pulls two cigars from his pocket and drops into the chair. He holds one out to me, and I take it.

"Think for two seconds, of all the stops you could pull to make this the most incredible experience for her. How you could go above and beyond to shock her with your thoughtfulness, because that's what you need to do—be fucking thoughtful. Listen. Think. Do one better. And sometimes . . . sometimes you might have to compromise or sacrifice things that mean something to you in order to show Indy that you're sincere. Because if you're not sincere in this whole fucking thing, what's the point?"

I roll the cigar in my hand while I mull over his words, thinking of all the things I could do that would fix what I've obviously fucked up.

Clearly, my silence lasts too long for Karas's short measure of patience.

"Are you going to do this or not? I need to know what the

fuck to tell Riscoff about the deal." He pulls out his cutter and snips off the end of his cigar before handing the cutter to me. "We can always go looking at Chinese steel, or gut our profits completely to buy North American."

"Let me win back my wife first. Then we'll worry about the deal."

Karas's cigar tilts in his mouth as he grins. "Good fucking answer. Hopefully, she doesn't kill you as soon as she sees you."

INDIA

Seventeen phone calls later, there's a boat on its way to get me. Forge must have told his employees that I'm a flight risk, because they're all out patrolling the grounds and the pier, and Dorsey has latched onto me like a barnacle to one of her boss's ships.

"Are you sure you're not hungry? You haven't eaten anything today. I'd be happy to have a nice lunch whipped up for you."

Considering this is about the tenth time she's made such an offer, my patience is waning.

I turn and give her a polite smile. "Still not hungry."

The hopeful expression on her face crumples like she's lost a battle. "Can we talk frankly for a moment, Mrs. Forge?" Dorsey swallows and threads her fingers together at her waist.

"It's Indy, please. And feel free to say whatever you need to say."

"Indy, have you ever had a job before that you couldn't afford to lose?"

I have no idea where she's going with this, but I nod.

"For me, this is that job. Working for Mr. Forge personally is a chance of a lifetime. He grooms all the people who
move up the ladder in his company, and gives them amazing
opportunities once they prove their loyalty and willingness to
do whatever it takes to complete a job well."

I study the woman with her strained posture and flexing
fingers. I know she's making a point, but I'm also trying to
keep my attention on the blue waters surrounding the island
and the boat that should be arriving any minute to get me out
of here.

"Dorsey, what's your point?" I ask as I focus beyond her,
but she sidesteps so she's directly in my line of sight.

"If you leave this island before Mr. Forge returns, we all
lose our jobs. Every single one of us."

I jerk my head back. "What?"

Dorsey bites her lip before continuing to speak. "I'm not
trying to guilt trip you into staying, but those were your
husband's orders. I don't agree with keeping a person somewhere they don't want to be, but if you could just not get on
that boat I know you're waiting for, I would be very grateful,
as would every other woman and man on this island."

Emotion fills her eyes, and all that hope and pleading may
as well be a sword shoved in my gut.

"I don't know what you're dealing with, but please,
before you leave, just . . . consider that more than your fate is
in your hands."

She gives me a weak smile and turns to walk back into
the house, leaving me standing with a duffel bag and my
rescue in sight . . . but my conscience rears its ugly head.

Fuck.

The white center-console fishing boat approaches, and I
have only a few minutes to make my decision. I heft the
duffel bag on my shoulder and cross the pool deck toward the
steps that lead down the cliffs. The steps that will take me far

away from here and . . . cost every single person on this island their job.

Damn you, Forge. This isn't fair.

I try to harden my heart. This isn't about them. This is about *me* and *my life.*

My phone vibrates with a text from Ruccio, the Italian wannabe professional poker player who had a boat and the time to come pick me up—in exchange for an hour of poker lessons so he can try to make the pro tour. Since he missed it six times already, I don't think an hour of my time is going to do the trick, but it was the price I had to pay to get what I needed.

"Please, before you leave, just . . . consider that more than your fate is in your hands."

Dammit, Dorsey's guilt trip was delivered much too effectively, because my feet stall.

And that's when I see the other boat. The black one. It looks like a shark cutting through the water like a knife, gaining on Ruccio's boat so quickly that it might just beat him to the dock.

Dorsey only said they'd lose their jobs if I left the island *before* Forge came back. If I leave after he arrives, then he can't follow through on his threat.

My feet come unstuck from the floor and I rush for the stairs. Something's wrong with my eyes, though, because they burn, and it's not from the wind whipping off the sea. No, they're burning from the ridiculous urge to cry.

Because my marriage, regardless of how fake it was, is over.

And somehow, again, regardless of whether it mattered . . . that reality strikes deep into the heart of me. *I failed at marriage.* But it wasn't real. It was never supposed to be real.

It doesn't matter. Forge doesn't care about me. All he cares about is his precious business deal.

It's the harsh truth, and I accept it for what it is.

I also make a promise to myself—I'm never getting married again. *Ever.* With that vow, I shore up that wall around my heart, mentally stacking the bricks and smearing a layer of concrete over the entire thing before adding sheets of Kevlar.

My heart is off-limits.

Goliath stands at the end of the dock. I wonder if he's waiting for Forge or if they left the biggest guy on the island as the last line of defense to keep me here. I'm honestly not sure which, because he has his back to me as I walk down the pier toward him.

Ruccio's ginger hair blows in the wind, and his wide smile is in place when he catches sight of me. He waves, and I lift a hand in a weak imitation of excitement, because I can also see Forge.

His dark features seem more forbidding than ever. There's no question he knows exactly what I'm planning to do. The bow of his boat lifts slightly as he pushes it faster, the sleek black tender cutting through the water like it's no opposition at all, and it noses ahead of Ruccio. The Italian doesn't realize he's racing, because he's backing off the throttle as Forge hammers his down.

I tighten my grip on the duffel bag and brace myself for the coming confrontation.

FORGE

I haven't lost her yet.

That's the only thought on my mind as I engage every one of the 3700 horsepower that is harnessed in the massive engines of the Black Shiver. A Boston Whaler heads for the pier, where Indy's blond hair whips around her shoulders, but I'm not going to let her leave without giving myself one last chance to fix this.

They always say you don't realize the value of what you have until you lose it, and before India Baptiste, I would have sworn I wasn't the kind of man who could be accused of that. But I am. I'm not infallible. I'm as fucking human as it gets.

I turn the boat, carving through the water, the steering wheel gripped tight in my palms. *Come on. Come on.*

After Karas's come-to-Jesus talk, I know he's right. If I want a shot at making this marriage real, I have to change how I think and what I do.

I've failed plenty of times in my life, but one thing I've never done is *quit.* I won't let Indy walk away without a fight.

I shoot past the Boston Whaler as I veer toward the dock, letting off the throttle at the very last second, and coast up to the pier. The rub-rail of the Shiver gently bounces off the padded pylons as it connects.

Indy, dressed in cut-off jean shorts and a pink tank top, jerks her head from me to the Boston Whaler and then back to the Shiver. When the dark-haired woman rises from the passenger seat next to me and becomes visible for the first time, Indy's eyes go wide.

She sets her jaw and her blue gaze turns frosty. "I expected a lot of things from you, Forge, but I didn't expect you to find a replacement that quickly." Her tone is even more frigid than her eyes. She shakes her head, the duffel bag on her shoulder swinging with her movement. "It's a good thing I was already planning on getting out of your way."

Goliath finishes tying up my tender, and I hop onto the dock as her escape vessel approaches.

"No, that's not what this is at all," I say, my words coming out gruff.

Indy looks away, her attention shifting to the captain of the other boat like she's already dismissed my existence. "I don't care what it is," she replies, still giving me the side of her face instead of her eyes. "I'll be gone in two minutes."

The boat coasts up to the dock, piloted by some ginger fuck.

"Signorina! Your knight in shining armor is here!"

He laughs, and my first instinct is to jump on board his boat and beat him within an inch of his life for daring to try to take what's mine. But I know that's not going to help the situation.

Indy takes one step toward the other boat, and I move into her path.

"I'm sorry. I fucked up. I shouldn't have tried to stop you." It's the most honest and sincere thing I can say, and the absolute truth.

Her chin juts out in that stubborn way of hers, and her

skeptical stare finally cuts to my face. "It doesn't matter anymore. This whole thing was a terrible idea to begin with. I was desperate. I would've married anyone to save my sister. That's on me. It doesn't matter that I was only ever a means to an end for you. I'm doing what needs to be done. It's time to end this farce."

She moves like she's trying to step around me, and I move with her.

I reach out to touch her but stop myself when she jumps back. My fingers flex in protest, but I know I earned her reaction, and I have to fucking fix this.

"Give me one more fucking chance. Please."

Her head tilts down, but her blue eyes are rimmed with red.

I hate that I fucking made her cry. I want to erase the lines on her brow that reveal the toll this has taken on her.

"Why should I?" she whispers.

"Because you're not a means to an end anymore. You're inside me. In my head. In the blood running through my fucking veins." I clear my throat and take a small step toward her. "If you go, you take all that with you, along with my fucking sanity."

Her eyelids flutter and her chin trembles, and I pray that I've made my case. But Indy bites down on her lip as her gaze slides past me to the Shiver.

"Who the hell is she?"

I totally forgot about the woman I begged to come with me. I whip around to acknowledge her.

"This is Sofia Russo. She's here from Milan to outfit you with dresses for the grand prix in Prague. That is, if you'll allow me to accompany you."

*M*y gaze skips between Forge and Sofia Russo. As soon as he said her name, I recognized her. She's not some hot young thing he brought to replace me in his bed before it was barely cold. She's a ridiculously famous designer, and Summer's always gone crazy over her dresses. She begged me to buy her one once, but even I couldn't swallow the five-figure price tag for a *dress*. The biggest stars are always wearing her designs on the red carpet.

And Forge brought her here with dresses for the grand prix.

There has to be a catch. I step forward until we're toe-to-toe.

"What's your angle, Forge? What the hell are you getting out of this?"

Even as I ask the question, I know the answer won't be the one I want to hear—that he'd do anything to keep me. That he's wildly in love with me and doesn't want to live without me. That he wants the kind of relationship Creighton and Holly have. A partnership. Something that will stand the test of time.

That's not us. We're not in love.

But as I think it, something pangs near my heart. *Maybe that's not the whole truth.* I feel something for him too that I've never felt for anyone else.

"You're my angle," he replies.

His dark brows dive together and a *V* forms between them. His gray eyes remind me of storm clouds rolling in over the sea.

"I don't want to be the man who only realizes what he had when it's gone. And that doesn't have a single fucking thing to do with any deal. I can buy steel from other people. It doesn't have to be your father. If you never want to meet him or see him or speak to him, that's your decision. All I want is a chance to make this right."

Forge pauses to take a breath, and my emotions are rioting as he speaks. But he's not done. He reaches out and brushes his knuckles across my jaw, and my lips tremble.

"I fucking care about you, Indy. Talk is cheap, but I'm not. I'm going to prove it to you. I want you to shine, and I'm going to do everything I can to make it happen. That's my angle."

My heart thunders, but I force myself to breathe calmly, even as his words chip away at the layers of concrete and Kevlar around my heart. Even as I tell myself not to believe him because he's cagey and withholds the truth. But the rough edge of his tone screams sincerity.

He's not bluffing.

"Indy?" This time it's Ruccio speaking my name.

I look over at the redhead. "Sorry. I'm just . . ."

"Ah, *bella.*" Ruccio smiles. "You're just listening to a man all but profess his love in a way that makes me wish he was talking to me instead."

One arm raised, I thread my fingers through my wind-whipped hair, not sure what the hell to do. I feel like I'm standing in a Robert Frost poem, but instead of two roads diverging in the woods, I've got two boats parked at a dock.

If I get in one, I know I'll be losing something I may never have a chance to get back. But if I choose to stay and believe what Forge says is true, I'm putting my heart at risk, and I know better than to bet more than I can afford to lose.

But if I win . . . I swallow before meeting his tumultuous gray gaze. *It could be everything.*

I can't let down my guard yet, though. I choose my words carefully to respond.

"Why should I believe you? How do I know that this isn't just another elaborate ruse to keep me under your thumb? A way to get what you want?"

Forge pulls his phone from his pocket, taps on the screen, and holds it out in front of him. "I'll call your father right now and tell him the deal is off."

Again, it could be a ploy. I step forward and take it out of his hand. The screen reveals the contact info for Grigory Federov.

My father.

I touch the screen to initiate the call. Forge's expression is impassive as the phone rings.

"This is Federov."

Oh my God, that's my father. His voice is deep and thickly accented.

Goose bumps rise on my arms as I let it wash over me. There's no question that he's Russian, which is so strange, because I don't feel Russian. I just feel like . . . me. A lump rises in my throat as Forge reaches for the phone. I know that if I let him take it, he will do everything he said.

"Forge?"

I tap the screen to end the call just as Forge's fingertips touch the phone.

"*Dio mio*, the anticipation is killing me, Indy. Are you going to stay with him or not?" Ruccio asks.

"I also wonder this," Sofia Russo says from the black boat where she holds a garment bag. "And not only because I have my newest designs at your disposal."

The phone vibrates in my hand, and Forge and I lock eyes. It's my father calling back. *My father.* The reason Forge married me, but not the reason he wants me to stay. My head screams at me to run, but my heart begs me to grab my husband and never let go.

"What do you want me to tell him, Indy? It's up to you."

I take a deep breath and make my decision, hoping like hell it's one I can live with. "Apologize for calling him by accident."

Forge sucks in a deep breath. "You won't regret this. I swear it on Isaac's grave."

*S*he still doesn't trust me. It's obvious as the jet takes off, bound for Prague.

Indy's pretending I don't exist, even as she sits across from me, flipping through a stapled sheaf of papers. It's been her MO since she thanked her friend for coming to her rescue and apologized for wasting his time. After he left, she led Sofia Russo down the pier with her head held high and her shoulders back, just like she was fucking royalty.

India Forge is absolutely incredible, and coming this close to losing her taught me an important lesson. *It's something I never want to risk again.*

Although, I haven't made much progress in getting her to unbend. I've never experienced such an uncomfortable silence in our lavish surroundings at the rear of the jet. Goliath, Donnigan, Bates, and Koba sit up front, no doubt feeling the awkwardness as well. I considered leaving Koba at home, but I decided I'd rather keep a close eye on him until I've either confirmed or refuted my earlier suspicions.

"Can I get you a drink, sir? Madam?" the flight attendant asks politely, and Indy looks up.

"Coffee. Black."

"Scotch. Neat. Thank you, Monique."

The flight attendant moves away to prepare our drinks, and I focus on Indy. "What are you doing?"

Her attention stays firmly on the papers in front of her. "Studying the list of players. Trying to remember who I've played before. I usually have more time to prepare, but this'll have to do."

"I can help."

This finally gets me eye contact. "Unless you have a list of their tells, then you can't."

Monique returns with our drinks, and I swirl my favorite vintage of Scotch in the glass. "Is that usually what you do? Study the players?"

"Of course," Indy replies, taking a sip of her coffee and then wincing when it hits her tongue. "Hell, I used to make flash cards of faces and write everything about them on the back. Details about their kids, wives, dogs, drinks, and obviously all their strengths and weaknesses at the table."

"Play the man, not the game," I reply as I lift my glass to my lips.

When Indy sets her coffee mug aside, I'm grateful she's allowing it to cool, because I didn't like seeing even that little discomfort on her face. *Yep, that's where I am. Well and truly fucked if I can't win her back.*

"Exactly. I'm not arrogant enough to think that I have this superior skill at poker that magically makes the right cards appear in front of me. If I had that, I wouldn't need to know anything about the person across the table."

The plane shudders briefly as it hits a patch of turbulence, and I lower my Scotch. "I know a lot of people. Try me."

Indy tucks one leg beneath her and her teeth clamp down on the end of the pen in her hand. "Not yet. I'm going to work through this, and I'll circle everyone I'm not familiar with. Then you can tell me what you know."

"I'm at your disposal, Mrs. Forge." I lean forward with the glass dangling from my fingertips. "Always."

At least that gets me a sharp look before she dismisses me completely for the rest of the flight.

INDIA

I've been to Prague before, but it was under much different circumstances. For starters, I didn't arrive in a private jet that was met by a chauffeur-driven blacked-out SUV.

No, back then we struggled through the crowd after jumping off a packed train, and Mom immediately got lost because she didn't speak Czech. Actually, she spoke English and German primarily at home, but both were shit compared to her Russian, which she only used if she was pissed.

Now it makes more sense. I don't know why I didn't question it as a kid. Probably because I was too busy worrying about where our next meal would come from.

Why did she run from my father? It's a question that's been plaguing me, but I'm not ready to ask it yet. The answer changes nothing now, and I have more important things to worry about—like the game ahead of me.

As we drive from the private airfield into the brightly lit streets of the city, the architecture is familiar. As a child, it seemed so ornate and royal to me because I didn't know anything but a hand-to-mouth existence and was quickly learning to live by my wits.

Which is exactly what I plan to do this time too.

Forge sits in silence beside me, and I'm not sure if that's for my benefit or his. Any trace of the easiness that existed between us before our fight is gone completely, and in its place is an awkward stiffness that I don't know how to banish, or even if I want to.

I know if I start to let him in again, it won't be partway. That's not how he's built. He's an all-or-nothing kind of man, and quite frankly, that terrifies me. If I give him that kind of access, he'll have the power to destroy me.

Marriage shouldn't be a minefield, but that's exactly what ours is.

"I secured us a penthouse at the event hotel. I thought you'd prefer convenience rather than staying somewhere more opulent."

I glance at him on the left side of the vehicle. Goliath sits up front with Donnigan, and Koba and Bates follow behind us in a second SUV.

"Thank you. I appreciate that. I prefer to waste as little energy as possible when I play, so staying there makes my life easier."

"If there's anything else I can do to help you, all you have to do is ask."

He sounds so . . . amenable, which puts me on guard. His face is cleanly shaven, and I wonder if that was for my benefit since I've never seen him like that before. He's always had that swarthy piratical look about him, and I'd obviously grown too attached to it.

As I drag my attention away from things that shouldn't matter, another question occurs to me. "What about your work and your schedule?"

"What's the point of being CEO if you can't have flex-ibility?"

It's not exactly the *nothing's more important than you* answer I was hoping for, but maybe that makes him a good CEO, as opposed to a shitty one who's willing and eager to run from his duties.

He leans back in the seat and continues. "I've also dele-gated everything possible to free up my time to be at your disposal for this event. Whatever you need, I'll take care of it."

Okay, so maybe I jumped to conclusions too soon.

"You don't need to trouble yourself. I'm here. You ensured my wardrobe will cause plenty of distraction at the table, and all I need to do is stay focused and play smart."

"I have faith that you'll do exactly that."

I look away from his intense gaze and out the window. "I guess we'll see," I say, but my response is clipped.

The SUV slows in front of a grand-looking hotel, and Forge leans toward me. I catch a hint of his sandalwood cologne, and my body is altogether too aware of his prox-imity and his scent. *And by too aware, I mean I like it too damned much.*

I don't know whether to trust this new version of the man I married. Until I have a better handle on it, I'm determined to protect my bruised heart.

I check the time on my phone and see we have four hours until the welcome reception begins. This may be an unsanc-tioned event, but the organizers have ensured it includes enough pomp and circumstance to impress the participants into parting with the hefty $100,000 entry fee, which is astro-nomical when compared to the other tournaments that take place all over the world.

This one also doesn't follow traditional rules, and doesn't include the preliminary qualifications because it's invitation-only. We'll play according to the rules the organizers set, which means two days of elimination games, and then a final evening with the top players. It doesn't matter how good a player is, we all start at the exact same place and must fight for survival and our seat at the final table.

Under other circumstances, I would be confident that I'll have one of those chairs, but I haven't had enough time to do all the homework that I would normally do.

I'm going to be fine. I'll learn quickly, and I'll win.

The valet attendant wearing a red jacket with gold braid opens my door and smiles. "Welcome, Mrs. Forge. We've been awaiting your arrival."

FORGE

*O*ther than the hour it takes for the makeup artist to enhance Indy's naturally beautiful features and the hair stylist to turn her blond hair into a sleek arrangement, Indy spends the entire time before the welcome reception with her gaze glued to her laptop as she watches video footage of the different players. I check my email for the dozenth time, and what I've been waiting for still hasn't come through. But it will, or heads will roll.

Indy has barely spoken to me, and I hate it.

I make myself a promise as she disappears into the bathroom to change into her dress. *If I can't earn her complete trust, I will let her go.*

It's a promise that will shred me to keep, but I have no other choice. However, it doesn't mean I won't do every goddamned thing in my power to prove to her that she can have everything she wants out of life with me at her gorgeous side.

It's the strangest fucking thing in the world. I've never had to prove my worth to someone—at least, not since those early days aboard ship when I feared Isaac would send me back if I couldn't pull my weight.

This woman, this complex, mysterious creature, has made the ground shift beneath my feet in a way I never thought possible.

When she opens the door from the en-suite bathroom and steps out on sky-high heels, I nearly swallow my tongue. She's wearing white, and I immediately picture what she would have looked like as a bride, walking down the aisle to me, if this marriage had started off differently.

"Jesus Christ."

Indy looks at me when I grate the words out under my breath. "What? Is something wrong?" She glances around the room as if scanning for a threat.

But of course, there isn't one, unless you count my urge to strip the dress off her and miss the welcome reception completely. *But that's not what we're here for. This is about her.*

"You look . . . beautiful." My voice roughens as I pay her the simple compliment that doesn't begin to do her justice.

She's a fucking siren. A goddess. And she doesn't even realize it.

Indy drops her gaze to her dress and then lifts it back at me. "As long as it makes them forget how good I am at the table, then it'll do."

I can't help but smile at her response. To Indy, her drop-dead-gorgeous appearance is a tool to be deployed strategically, which should have been just one more clue that she's the only woman who could flip my entire world upside down.

"Then by all means, let's go make them forget how dangerous you really are."

WE ENTER THE RECEPTION, which is already in full swing, with waiters moving with flutes of Cristal and canapés through the gamblers and guests milling around the blue water of an Olympic-size swimming pool. Immediately, I start looking for the players on the list I borrowed from Indy.

Over a hundred card players are here, including all of Europe's best, all after the extravagant pot and bragging rights. Only two of the twenty top players are women, and one of them is my wife.

As Indy engages in conversation with people she knows, I step back and let her lead. I'm here for her.

"Part of me wondered if you would let her come," a Russian-accented voice remarks from beside me, and I turn my head to see Belevich.

"You clearly don't know my wife if you think she needs my permission to do anything." As soon as I say the words, I realize it's the honest truth. There's nothing I could stop her from doing if she set her mind to it. I tried and failed at that already.

He grunts as Indy steps a few more feet away from me to hug a woman I don't recognize. I remember what she said about memorizing details of opponents' lives, down to their wives, kids, and dogs. She doesn't just deploy that information at the table as she's playing. No, she uses it to charm everyone with more effectiveness than I've ever experienced.

"You Americans don't know how to handle women. You should keep a tight leash on her. Someone is bound to try to steal her away from you, if you're not careful," Belevich warns.

Summoning my self-control, I turn to face him, using the bulk of my frame to tower over him. "Someone like who? You?"

He smooths his blond goatee, camouflaging his sly grin.

"I don't have a wish to be ruined slice by slice like you've been doing to de Vere. She isn't worth it."

That's where he's fucking wrong. She's worth everything.

I'm not about to correct him, though. Belevich doesn't need any additional incentive to go gunning for Indy beyond trying to beat her at poker.

"But not everyone thinks like me, Forge. Not everyone is as smart. Remember that."

Belevich slips away, and I step forward in the crowd and position myself at Indy's back.

"Yes, yes, I did get married. Amazing how fast news travels in small circles, isn't it?" She turns around as if looking for me, and her lips form a small *o* as she sees me standing behind her. "Mrs. Benedetto, this is my husband, Jericho Forge."

I incline my head at the older woman who rests her hand on the arm of a stocky man in a tux. "It's a pleasure to meet you both."

"I've heard of you," the Italian man says. "You're in ships."

"What a handsome man. Such a catch. You did well, my dear." Mrs. Benedetto lifts her champagne flute. "Cheers."

Indy clinks glasses with her.

"Yes, in shipping," I say as I slide my arm around Indy's waist. "But she's the catch, not me." Indy stiffens slightly within my hold. "I assure you, I'm the lucky one in this marriage."

"Oh, and his flattery is effortless. Hold on tight to that one, India."

INDIA

*W*e move away from the Benedettos, and I've already lost my patience for tonight. I want to get the hell out of here and back to our room so I can watch more video footage, but I know I can't make an early exit without making people talk. It's like playing chicken. Most of the players, the smart ones, would rather not be here, but no one is willing to leave first because it's a sign of weakness.

Or at least, that's what I tell myself, and it's the only reason I made sure I came.

Forge lifts a glass of champagne off a tray. He looks unbelievable in a tux, but there's no chance of the formal wear civilizing him completely. His long black hair brushes the white collar, and the gold of his earring winks when it catches the light. The five o'clock shadow already shades his strong jaw, and every time I catch a glimpse of him, my mouth goes dry and I'm reminded that I've got nothing on under this dress.

Nipples, down.

When he holds the champagne out to me, I wave him off.

"I don't need to be tipsy. I have too much work to do after we get the hell out of here."

He wraps my fingers around it anyway. "Don't drink it. Just hold it. It's part of networking. If everyone else has a drink in their hand, you look suspicious without one and make them rethink how much *they're* drinking. Which is exactly the opposite of what you want. You want them walking into the games tomorrow with their heads pounding and stomachs sour from too much booze."

He makes a point, one that I should have thought of myself. "How do you know so much?"

"I live and breathe strategy." He winks at me, which makes him look even more piratical.

"You could be playing, you know. I'm sure the organizers would fall all over themselves to kick someone off the roster to add your name. You're better than almost everyone here, but you know that too."

He lifts his own drink to his lips and takes a sip. "I could. But that's not why I'm here. This is your game. I'm just arm candy at best, and a distraction at worst."

His droll tone while referring to himself as arm candy is too much. My entire body shakes as a belly laugh bubbles up from deep down.

"Is that what you are? Arm candy?" I lift my other hand to my face, trying to cover my mirth before I draw too much attention to myself.

Forge grins widely, and the smile threatens to split his face in two. "Damn right, and I'm good at it. Now, let's go charm these guys into thinking you're not the most lethal player they've ever faced."

AN HOUR LATER, Forge has proven his worth and commitment to me at least a half dozen times over.

He let me lead, let me play the role I set for myself this evening. Almost as if on my signal, he charmed the women, disarmed the men, and made me feel like we're untouchable as a team.

When we step away from yet another couple's congratulations on our marriage, the sound of the string quartet floats over us as we stand at the edge of the pool.

I step closer to his side and give in to my urge to inhale the scent I've quickly become addicted to. "For a man who I thought hated small talk and polite conversation, you're really good at this."

He rests a hand on the small of my back, and it feels so perfectly natural. Actually, just *perfect.*

"I wouldn't do it for anyone but you." He holds up his arm and glances at his watch. "Are you ready to leave? I think we've stayed long enough to prove your point."

"How did you know?"

The golden outdoor lights lend a warmth to his tanned complexion and glint off his shiny black locks as he leans down to whisper in my ear. "I'm learning you."

Before I can think of something to say in response, glass shatters as it hits the cement a few feet away, and a waiter tumbles toward us, his tray flying at my head. I jerk sideways to avoid it and lose my balance, and the tray and I go careening toward the water.

Forge's arms wrap around me, but even his strength can't overcome the laws of physics. We plunge beneath the surface together in a massive splash of thankfully warm water.

In a split second, I'm pulled to the surface and suck in a breath.

"Are you okay?" he asks.

I nod, wiping the water from my eyes in a way that I'm sure will leave me looking like a drowned raccoon.

Forge frowns, sliding his palms up and down my arms as if checking me for injury. Although his black hair sticks to his forehead, hanging in his eyes, he gives no thought to righting himself. The bespoke tuxedo he's wearing had to cost a small fortune, but he doesn't give it a single thought.

His only concern is me.

"I'm fine. Just . . . wet." I look down at myself, and my hair flops forward again into my face.

The entire crowd stares wide-eyed at us in the pool, and I can't help it. I burst out laughing. The worry on Forge's face fades away as my shoulders shake, and a smile crosses his face and a deep rumble emanates from his chest.

"We look ridiculous," I say as tears slip from my eyes and my laughter continues.

He pushes my hair out of my face and uses both thumbs to wipe under my eyes. "You're still beautiful."

FORGE

I follow her through the water to the steps that lead out of the pool, and a man is wringing his hands nearby.

"Sir, I'm so sorry. One of the waitstaff tripped. We apologize wholeheartedly for the inconvenience. Are either of you injured? We can send for a doctor."

"We're fine, but thank you," Indy replies as she walks up the steps ahead of me.

The man's eyes go wide with shock, noticing one fact before I do. Indy's white dress is now completely transparent. "Is there anything—"

"We'll take your jacket, sir."

He straightens and then nods like a puppet. "Of course."

Indy looks down, and I know the exact moment she realizes she looks completely naked. "Of all the times I chose to wear white." Her tone is still filled with mirth.

I snag the jacket out of the man's hands and wrap it around her. "Let's get you back to the room, Ace."

"I lost my shoes too."

I look down at her bare feet on the stonework surrounding the pool. "Someone else will get them. I've got you."

I lift her into my arms, and for the first time, Indy doesn't protest. Probably because she wants to get the fuck out of here as quickly as possible. I'll take it.

Like it's the Red Sea, the crowd parts and I carry her through, wrapped in another man's jacket. I would have offered her my own, but soaking wet as it is, it wouldn't have been the most chivalrous offer. Not that I've ever thought much on the topic of chivalry.

When we reach the elevator, she wiggles in my arms. "You can put me down. I can walk now."

"I know, but this is the least I can do since I couldn't save you from going in to begin with."

Thankfully, a smile forms on her lips. "I appreciate that you tried, but you didn't have to go in too. At least one of us would've been dry then."

"Where you go, I go. Even if it's overboard."

60

INDIA

*T*hey say actions speak louder than words, but tonight, Forge's actions and words are both equally loud. I'm really not sure what to think.

Actually, that's not true. If I'm being honest with myself, I know exactly what I want to think—that what he said at the pier on the island is true.

"Talk is cheap, but I'm not. I'm going to prove it to you. I want you to shine, and I'm going to do everything I can to make it happen."

His words echo in my head as we approach the room to see Batman and Koba standing outside the door. They both start down the hall toward us, but Forge waves them off.

"We fell in the pool. Everything's fine."

Bates straightens with a quick nod. "We heard, sir. Mrs. Forge's shoes are being retrieved."

"Thank you," I tell him. "Although I don't think I'm going to be wearing them anytime soon."

"I'll have them sent out for cleaning and repair, ma'am. If they can be salvaged, I'll have them returned to you."

I give him a grateful smile. "Thank you."

"We're in for the night. See that we're not disturbed." Forge delivers his order and Bates hurries to open the door, standing aside to let us enter. As soon as it shuts behind us, Forge lowers me to my feet.

"Let's get you out of these clothes."

I can't help but laugh. "Turning on the charm, I see," I say with a wink.

One side of his mouth quirks up. "I don't think there's enough charm in the world to get what I want from you, so I'll earn it the old-fashioned way."

"And what's that?"

"Patience."

I choke on the laugh that bursts from my lips. "I didn't think you knew the meaning of the word."

This time, Forge winks at me. "I'm learning a few things . . . like how to make you laugh." Thankfully, he disappears into the bathroom before he realizes I'm staring dumbfounded after him.

Who the hell is this man, and which one is the real Jericho Forge?

I hear the water turn on in the shower, and Forge returns, helping me remove the now soaked jacket from over my shoulders. I step into the bathroom, and when he follows behind me, I'm not sure if he intends to shower with me or not.

My nipples, already diamond points, turn harder at the thought, and I can't ignore the burst of heat between my legs.

I may not know which Jericho Forge is the real one, but there's never been any question that I'm desperately attracted to the entire package, even when it was against my will. It's not against my will anymore, though.

"Do you need help with your dress?" he asks.

"Please." I turn toward the mirror to give him my back and find him staring at me in the mirror. For the space of three heartbeats, we're both completely still as he watches me, watching him.

His Adam's apple bobs as he reaches for the tab of the zipper at the top of my spine. He slides it down slowly enough to be seductive, but then he backs away. "I'll leave you to your shower. Call for me if you need anything."

His eyes are still on mine as he takes another backward step toward the door. The devil riding my shoulder prompts me to speak.

"Aren't you stripping too?"

"I'll wait until you're done."

I release my hold on my dress and let it fall to a puddle on the floor. I lose his gaze for a moment as it follows my dress and then skims up my naked body, leaving a trail of heat in its wake.

"What if I don't want you to wait?"

His hands curl into fists at his sides before he flexes them. *He wants me as badly as I want him.*

"What game are you playing, Indy?"

I turn around to face him instead of his reflection and take two steps back until my ass hits the edge of the counter. "Only the ones I can win."

61

FORGE

*J*ndy hops up on the counter, completely naked, and I remember what I told her. *Patience. I'm being fucking patient.*

But when I see the silver piercing between her slick lips catch the light, I don't care if it's a game only she can win. I'll play.

I tear off my soaked tux and remove the studs from my shirt cuffs, dropping them to the floor in a *plink plink.* Once I've divested myself of my shirt and shoes, I walk toward her. The shower door is still open, and steam fills the bathroom.

Fucking hell, I want her.

I take one step, and then pause.

This tournament is about her. Not me getting my rocks off. There's nothing I want more than to sink into that tight pussy, but that's not going to prove how I feel about her.

"What's wrong?" she asks.

"Nothing." I turn off the shower, then close the distance between us, and her legs wrap around my hips. She pushes against me, but I pick her up instead and carry her out to the bed.

"But why—"

"I'm not fucking you tonight, India. Not because there's nothing more I'd rather do, but because if I start, we're going to stay up all night. And you have to play in the morning with a clear head and not be sleep deprived."

Two lines appear between her brows. "Excuse me?"

"This tournament is about *you*. That's how it's going to stay."

"So . . . you're turning me down?" Hurt colors her tone, which is exactly the opposite of my goal.

"No," I say as I lay her on top of the coverlet. "I'm going to eat your pussy until you come hard against my tongue, and then I'm going to send you back to the shower so you can rinse off. Then you're going to get to work."

With each word, her blue gaze widens further.

"Do you have a problem with that?"

Her mouth opens, and she stares at me like I'm a different man than the one she's used to. And maybe I am.

"I . . . I don't think I have a problem with that."

"Good, because that's what's fucking happening right now."

With a satisfied grin on my face, I proceed to do exactly as I promised, using my thumbs to spread her lips and lick from base to clit, then suck hard until her knees are no longer steady.

I eat her like she's the finest fucking delicacy I've ever tasted, because she is. I suck and lick and fuck her with my tongue until she grabs a pillow to muffle her screams.

When I pull back, my dick harder than an iron stake, her blue eyes are hazy. I crawl up the bed to press my lips to hers. I move to pull away, but she wraps a hand around my neck and tugs me back to kiss me harder and deeper.

It's the sweetest victory of my entire fucking life.

INDIA

a knock on the door comes after we've both showered, *separately,* and room service delivers our food.

He's my husband. So what if he ate my pussy and then sent me off to shower so I could get back to work?

Still, I can't stop thinking about the way he put me first, refusing to get himself off. The way he's put me first since the moment he made the vow to prove to me that I made the right choice by not leaving with Ruccio.

Forge rises from his steak to answer the door. When he pulls it open, Goliath hands him something.

"As you requested, sir."

"Thank you."

When he returns to the table, I stare at the tablet in his hands. "Did you forget something?"

He shakes his head as he sits down. "No, but I was hoping it would come sooner."

"What is it?"

Forge taps the screen a few times, and then hands the tablet across the table to me. "Video footage of every player here who's ever been filmed. There's also a list of all their known tells, plus the tells that my people have spotted while gathering the footage."

Holy. Fucking. Shit.

My heart slams into my chest as I stare at him in shock.

FORGE

*J*ndy's silverware clatters against the plate when it falls from her frozen fingers. Barefaced, her wet hair wrapped in a towel, and wearing a hotel robe, she looks about twenty years old.

"Are you fucking serious?"

"Of course." I point at the iPad in her hands. "It's all there."

She glances down and scans the screen before looking up at me again. "How . . . when . . . why?"

"Because you came to win, and I had the resources to gather the information you needed." I reach for the sparkling water between us and fill her glass.

"But . . . *how?*"

"I pay a lot of people very well to do what I ask them to do."

"I . . . I don't know what to say."

"You don't have to say anything. In fact, you have a hell of a lot of homework to catch up on before you need to get to sleep so you're rested for the morning." I pick up my fork as she continues to stare at me.

"I don't know how to thank you for this."

"No thanks necessary. I told you I'd make you shine, and that's what I'm doing."

INDIA

I don't know what to say or what to think. He completely blew me away. It's also the most thoughtful thing anyone has ever done for me in my life.

"Well, thank you anyway. This is incredible. Truly incredible."

I rise from the table, the food no longer holding any interest at all, and drop onto one of the four sofas in the penthouse suite.

Forge's silverware clicks as I tap on the first file, labeled MARTIN KRAUSE. He's one of the top favorites to win the whole tournament. That's when I realize the players' information isn't sorted alphabetically, but is in numerical order by their record and skill level.

Holy shit. Forge's people are good.

I delve into the information, reading Krause's only known tell, one that I've never heard anyone speak of. He stops moving his toothpick and lets it settle in the right side of his mouth when he's bluffing.

With my lip clamped between my teeth, I watch the first video clip. *Well, shit, I would never have guessed that.* The man constantly shifts his toothpick around, making it impossible to follow. The pause is nearly imperceptible, but it's there.

I file it away in my memory. Tomorrow morning, we all start out at ground zero. Players are seated randomly at the tables in such a way that it's totally possible, although highly unlikely, that every single heavy hitter could play at the same table in the very first round.

Closing the file, I open the next one.

Chen Yang. I played him once years ago when I was still in the underground circuit. He slaughtered the entire table, and I barely made it through the night holding on to my buy-in. I was never able to spot a single tell.

But there they fucking are, highlighted in yellow on the page in front of me. *He touches the corner of his mouth with the tip of his tongue for a moment before he bluffs. When he has a particularly good hand, he avoids looking at his cards for as long as possible, before checking one last time before he bets.*

It's a goddamned revelation.

Forge rises, and I look up. "Let me help."

"You've done plenty. I don't know how much you paid your people, but this is a gold mine. I just wish I had more time to study it all."

He looks down at his watch. "You should be asleep by two, no later. I had the files sent to me too. We'll divide and conquer. Tomorrow, before you sit every game, I'll give you a kiss for good luck, and tell you everything I've learned that you haven't."

My face hurts from the sheer magnitude of my grin. "It sounds like you're a goddamned genius."

"Not quite. It's teamwork. Together, we're unbeatable."

HOURS LATER, my head droops, and I lose my grip on the tablet. When it flops over in my lap, Forge scoops it up.

"That's enough for tonight. You need your sleep."

"Just a few more minutes," I say, fighting to open my eyes as I yawn.

"Sleep, Indy. I'll go through the rest. You'll be ready tomorrow. I promise."

Strong arms slide under my body and lift me.

I curl into his heat. "You need sleep too."

"I'm used to going without. I'll be fine."

"But—" Whatever I was going to say is silenced with the press of his lips on mine.

"Sleep, Ace. We got this."

65

FORGE

I've felt pride before. Like when I caught my first fish, and Isaac ruffled my hair and taught me how to clean and fry the fish for dinner. Or when I made my first purchase of a cargo ship, and Isaac beamed with approval. When my assets hit the billion-dollar mark, and I knew he'd be smiling down on me from above for being a good steward of his legacy.

But I've never felt pride like I do right now, watching Indy sweep her first game with the notorious Chen Yang at the table. The man's placid features stiffen with each hand, as he realizes there's nothing he can do to stop her. She's a beast. Cunning, yet brilliant in her strategy for betting and goading him, while handling the rest of the players at the table like they barely exist on her radar.

It's a master class in poker, and the crowd around the table has grown to the point where people are shoving to get a better look at Indy. Her dress, a bold purple satin number, is more suited for evening, but she wears it like royalty.

When the game ends, the other players at the table rise

and clap—all but Yang. He hangs his head in shame, a feeling he's probably not accustomed to dealing with.

Indy waves at the people watching, collects her chips, and steps away. Goliath is at her side instantly to take the trays, and she hands them off without a question as she scans the crowd for me. As soon as she sees me, standing just off to the side of the crowd where I could get a better view, the most dazzling smile stretches across her lips as she runs toward me, not missing a single step in her tall heels.

She launches herself at me. "I won! Against Chen!"

Joy, like I've never felt before, fills my entire being as I catch her with open arms, lifting her into the air.

"You didn't just win, you schooled the poor bastard so badly, he may never show his face again."

Indy lets out a squeal as I spin her around and carry her away from the encroaching crowd. Donnigan and Goliath keep them at a distance as we steal away to a corner.

I put Indy on her feet, and she bounces like a kid at Christmas.

"I can't fucking believe that just happened. First game."

"You made a hell of a splash." My cheeks hurt from smiling so hard for the last few hours as Indy destroyed Yang.

"I was torn. I could let him win, and stay a sleeper player, but too many people in this room already know me and my reputation. They've probably studied me like I'm studying them."

"So you said *fuck it* and crushed him?"

"Yes, and it felt incredible." She leans up and presses a kiss to my lips. "Thank you for making that possible."

I don't know if I'll ever get used to Indy kissing me without being asked, but I vow in that moment that I'll never take it for granted.

"It was all you, Ace." I wrap an arm around her waist.

"Let's get some food and water in you, and get you back down to play the next game."

THE MORNING SETS the tone for the rest of the day. Indy wins soundly at every table. She takes out one more favorite and wipes away plenty of mid-list hopefuls. No one in the room can tear their eyes off her, least of all me.

When the last card has finally been dealt, I sweep in to get her chips and hand them off to Goliath.

"You're about to be swamped with people who want to talk to you, and that's not what you need right now." I whisper it against her ear, picking up the subtle hint of citrus from her hair.

Her posture started to droop in the last game, and I know the daylong event has taken a toll on her, even if no one else would notice.

"Oh God, I don't want to talk to anyone. I'm talked out. My brain is *mush*."

I jerk my head at Goliath, and he and Donnigan form a protective barrier around us. "Then we'll get you to the room, and you can chill out in the tub."

"But I need to study too."

"You chill in the tub, and I'll help."

Instead of replying, she thanks me with another kiss that I add to my tally.

INDIA

*W*hen Bates opens the door to the penthouse, the scent of food makes my stomach rumble. Even though Forge has kept me fed and hydrated all day, the last game seemed endless. I've been dying for some quiet, and for my hands to be empty of cards and chips.

Forge pauses at the doorway, giving orders to the men before closing the door behind him.

I've already fallen on dinner like a ravenous beast, and I can't bring myself to care. Across the table from my heaping plate of pasta, Forge cuts into his steak with a grin. *Obviously, he doesn't mind either.*

"Oh, damn, this is good." Fresh veggies keep it light and crisp, but the sauce coating the chicken and noodles is delicious. I fork up another bite as I swallow.

"I ordered you two desserts. I wasn't sure if you were a chocolate fan. You picked berry ice cream when we went out with Holly and Karas, so I hedged my bets," he says before popping a piece of steak into his mouth.

"Dessert too? I just might keep you around, Forge." I toss out the comment like it's a joke, but it's not.

If *this* version of the man is anywhere close to his true self, I could get used to it. To him. To feeling like I matter. Like he values me and sees me for who I am and appreciates it.

I'm afraid to get caught up in all the feelings swirling around in my brain now, and instead, want to continue riding the high from my day of winning. I'm afraid that if I get too attached to this Forge, he'll disappear again when things aren't fun and games anymore.

I'm going to soak this up like it's a once-in-a-lifetime experience.

Forge pauses, his silverware still over his plate. He's staring at me like he wants to say something, but his lips don't move.

"Is something wrong?" I ask.

"No. Nothing. I'm proud of you, Indy. Proud as hell."

The words I didn't expect to hear come out in a smooth, genuine tone. They unleash a burning sensation in my eyes that I know foretells tears, and I blink a few times to keep them back.

When is the last time anyone but Alanna or Summer said they were proud of me? Never.

"I've had more fun in the last eighteen hours than I can remember having in years. Thank you for that. For showing me that there's more to life than my island and my boats and my business."

"Ships." I correct him like he did when speaking with Karas, and shoot him a wink to prevent my tears from falling. "And really?"

He lowers his silverware to the plate, and his hands grip the edge of the table. "I never planned on getting married, but I think that's because I never knew a woman like you existed. You're a once-in-a-lifetime find, India. I'm proud to be your husband."

Shit. The tears come, even though I don't want them to. I drop my fork to lift my napkin to my face to wipe them away.

"I didn't mean to—" He reaches for his napkin to offer it to me.

I wave him off before he can apologize. "It's not you. I just . . . I guess it's been a long, tough day, and my tear ducts decided they needed a workout too." I dab the tears away and lower the napkin.

"The last thing I ever want to do is make you cry. Whatever you believe about me, know that's a fact."

Once my tears are dry, I lay the napkin back on my lap. "I know that much. I may not have figured you out yet, but I do know that."

I walk into the final day of the grand prix wearing a gold mermaid-style dress from Sofia Russo that fits me like a second skin.

I may as well have a target on my back because everyone is watching me. My tactics have always relied on flying below the radar—because most male poker players tend to discount women—and if that failed, on distraction.

For this tournament, however, my tactics have changed. I feel like a wrecking ball instead, smashing through everything in my way, except more gracefully and better dressed.

Assignments are announced and Forge follows me to my table, with Donnigan and Goliath on either side of us. Wherever we go, people watch.

Before Forge, it would have driven me crazy, but now, I barely care.

We stayed up until two a.m., going over the remaining players and all their tells, and anything else that can help me today. I'm working very hard to keep my expectations low and my ego in check, which is hard after such big wins yesterday.

The table for the finals is set up in another room, and I'm going to earn my seat at it today. I rest my hands on the chair back that I'm going to take first, but when I close my eyes, I'm already visualizing standing up a winner and moving on to the next round. It's a little trick I learned years ago, and I was so flustered the night at La Reina, I forgot to do it . . . and I lost.

"Kick ass, Ace. You got this." Forge leans in to kiss my cheek, and I turn to give him my mouth instead.

Maybe I didn't lose that night at all. Maybe fate took charge and sent me down a new path. One that includes this man, who I'm no longer quite so scared to fall in love with. Maybe . . . maybe this can actually work.

When Forge pulls back, he has a smudge of red on his lips, and I reach up to wipe it away with my thumb. It feels like a very domestic move, and something about that makes me happy.

"Thank you."

"For what?" he asks as he presses a kiss to the pad of my thumb.

"Everything."

AFTER I WIN my semi-final game, Jericho picks me up and lifts me into the air, just like he's done every single time I've won since we arrived. It's part of my new routine for games that I'll happily continue.

We eat, and I have a longer break before the final starts tonight, so I go back to studying the players who will be seated at the table with me. Jericho excuses himself to take a phone call, and I can't help but wonder if it's my father.

Instead of being filled with anger and resentment, I'm

more curious than anything. *Do I want to meet him?* Is that even an option I'm willing to entertain?

I put it out of my mind as I go back to studying, because I don't want to distract myself from the remaining game standing in my way of victory. I haven't forgotten about Belevich's side bet either. If I keep kicking ass, I'm going to walk out of here an even wealthier woman. *Maybe Jericho will let me buy dinner then.*

Yes, he's Jericho again in my head. Which apparently is only a thing when I'm happy and not pissed at him. That's when he becomes Forge, which sounds just as hard as he can look when he's acting unreasonable.

He returns to the room, sliding the phone into the pocket of his charcoal-gray suit pants, and I can't quite read his guarded expression.

"Is everything okay?"

"It's fine."

"Did you close the deal?"

He continues toward me and crouches in front of where I'm curled up on the couch. "I'm not being patronizing when I say this, but don't worry about it right now. Keep your focus where it needs to be. We can talk about everything else tonight."

It's exactly the response I needed, but didn't know I needed until he said it. Again, I find myself thanking him, and appreciate him even more.

FORGE

"*A*re you ready?" I ask from the doorway of the bathroom where she touches up her lipstick, which I know will just end up on my lips or cheek, and I can't find it in myself to care.

Actually, if I were pressed, I'd probably say I fucking love it. Because as much as I like marking her for all to see, I love that she's leaving her mark too.

I also owe Karas a case of his favorite whiskey. I almost fucked up beyond repair, and he saved my ass with his advice and experience.

Indy turns to smile at me, her blond hair curling down around her shoulders, and the red on her lips is as bold as the woman wearing it.

"I'm as ready as I'll ever be. I've drilled every detail of their play into my head, and now I just want to go crush them and then celebrate with you . . . and the Kraken." She winks when she refers to my dick with her favorite nickname, and my chest shakes with laughter.

I know there's nothing I wouldn't do to keep her this happy . . . because it makes me fucking happy too.

"The Kraken and I agree that sounds like the perfect plan."

As she walks toward me, I pull a small box from my pocket that I had Bates fetch over lunch today.

"In the meantime, this is for you." I hold it out, and she blinks before looking down at the black velvet.

"What is it?"

"A gift."

She tilts her head as she looks back up at me. "What kind of gift?"

"The kind you open."

"Smartass," Indy murmurs before she finally takes it from me and flips open the lid to reveal two tanzanite studs that perfectly match the indigo color of her eyes. She releases a ragged breath, and I hope I didn't fuck up.

"Diamonds would've been the obvious choice, but I thought you'd like these better."

Her lips tremble before they stretch into a smile. "They're absolutely perfect. How did you know? Because I definitely like them better."

I remove the earrings from the cushions holding them in place and hold one out. "Because I'm learning you, and it's the most fascinating subject I've ever studied." When her hand shakes as she takes the earring from me, I realize I need to lighten the mood. "Not to mention occasionally frustrating, but always fuckable."

Her shoulders lift with her burst of laughter as she removes her gold earring and replaces it.

As soon as Indy's tanzanite studs are secured, I escort her down to the room where the finals will take place, ignoring my buzzing phone the entire way.

When we reach the door, Goliath taps my arm. He's looking down at his phone. "Sir, there's a call you need to take."

"Not now. Nothing is more important than this."

Indy turns and smiles at me with a wink. "Take your call, Jericho. Just don't miss the game. I want you to see me win."

INDIA

ith Goliath and Bates tailing me, I walk into the room. Belevich is standing along the perimeter, and I march toward him with my shoulders back, boobs out, and feeling utterly unstoppable.

"You've played well, Mr. Belevich."

The Russian casually sips on what I assume is his trademark glass of Beluga Noble vodka. "Not as well as you, Mrs. Forge." He looks around. "Where did your husband run off to?"

I lift my hand to one of my new earrings and smile. "He'll be right back. Don't worry."

"He seems to be your lucky charm. I'd hate for you to lose him now."

Something about Belevich's tone sets alarm bells ringing in my head and a chill skittering down my spine. "What the hell do you mean?"

The Russian sips again, the gold signet ring on his pinky winking in the light. "Nothing. Just that I hope it works out for you both. But I hope more that I walk away the winner of our bet."

A rush of air comes from behind me, and I turn to see four men in black suits who look like they must be private security for another high-roller player file out the door. Goliath follows a short distance behind them, leaving only Bates waiting in the wings for me to finish my chat with Belevich. I search for Jericho, but I don't see him.

"Don't stare at them so closely. You don't want their attention," Belevich says in a low voice, and I cut my gaze back to him.

"What are you talking about?"

"Those men that your security is following. He shouldn't be following them. He should walk the other way."

What the fuck is going on? The chills I felt moments ago spread across my skin as Goliath disappears.

"Who the hell are they?"

"Bratva. One of them was playing but lost the last round to me." Belevich grunts and looks like he's proud of that fact.

"Shouldn't you be worried about them more than me or Goliath?"

He tugs down the collar of his starched white shirt just far enough for me to see the outline of a wing tattooed on his neck. That's when I remember the rumors that have floated around on Ibiza about Belevich's connections to the Russian mob.

"Of course not." His Russian accent thickens. "At least, not over something like this."

"Where are they going?" I swallow, trying to stop the tendrils of fear wrapping around me from growing stronger.

"Probably to drink vodka." He lifts his glass as though in salute, and I force a paltry smile.

Is he just fucking with me? Trying to throw me off my game? Of course he is, and I'm fucking falling for it.

I back away from Belevich with a nod that says *I see what the fuck you're doing and it's not going to work.*

"I'll see you at the table, Belevich."

"Likewise, Queen Midas."

I try to flush out all my uneasy feelings by focusing on my breathing, but they don't abate completely. Goliath returns to the room, but there's no sign of Jericho.

Something's wrong. But wouldn't Goliath be with Jericho then? I glance over my shoulder to look at the giant with dreadlocks, but he stays perfectly still, giving me nothing.

I'm overreacting. Nothing's wrong. Jericho's just running late.

The cards are dealt and I settle into the game, tuning out everything else but the other players.

I won. I won. I fucking won!

I jump out of my chair and spin around to rush into Jericho's arms . . . but he's not there. Goliath is gone too. Bates sweeps in to grab my chips as everyone crowds around me, cheering and popping bottles of Dom.

From across the table, Belevich lifts his now-empty glass of vodka the tiniest bit. He folded early in the final hand, which surprised me then, but I couldn't care less now.

"Where is Forge?" I ask Bates, dread curling in my belly. "He said he'd be here. Did I miss him?"

Bates shakes his head. "No. I think something came up. Goliath went to go check on him about twenty minutes ago so he wouldn't miss the last hand. I don't know what the fuck happened to him either."

Dread is now thrumming through my veins with every beat of my heart.

I grip Bates's arm. "Something's wrong. He wouldn't miss the game. Not after all this."

"Mrs. Forge, I can't leave you. Those are my orders."

I squeeze him tighter. "I'm giving you orders *now.* Go

find my fucking husband before I fire you myself." I release my grip and stop short of giving him a shove.

"Mrs. Forge—"

"I'm perfectly safe in a roomful of people, and I'm about to accept a big fat check on TV." My tone is clipped because I've lost my goddamned patience. "Nothing is going to happen to me if you go find him and get your ass back in here in the next ten minutes. Now, take my chips and *go.*"

Bates wants to argue, but the organizer of the grand prix pushes between us, holding out a crystal flute bubbling with champagne. A commentator follows behind, carrying a microphone, and begins asking me questions about my play and how I feel after winning such a prestigious tournament.

I have absolutely no idea what I'm saying to either of them because my brain is running a million miles per hour in the other direction. I keep it short and sweet, smiling for the camera as I accept the giant check. When I finally step offstage into the mob, Bates still isn't back.

What the fuck is going on?

I push through the crowd, shaking hands and using the check as a shield until I reach the elevator and smash the button for the penthouse.

Thankfully, I stuck a keycard for the suite in my small clutch, along with my lipstick for touch-ups. Panic doesn't strike until I step out of the elevator on the penthouse level and see two men sprawled on the carpet ahead of me.

"No!" I sprint down the hallway, skidding to a halt beside Bates, whose neck is at an awkward angle.

Oh, sweet fucking Jesus. He's dead. *He's dead.*

I rush to the next form. It's Donnigan. I check for a pulse. He's dead too.

Tears burn my eyes as I swipe the key to open the door.

"Jericho!"

I scan the living room. It's completely trashed. Tables are

upturned, and the mirror over the console table is smashed. Traces of dark red are mixed in the shattered glass fragments.

Goliath is facedown on the floor, and a dark stain spreads out on the carpet beside him.

"No! No!"

I stand up and whirl around, my head spinning faster than my body as I stumble into the bedroom. It's a mess too. The bedspread is missing, and there's a dark stain on the rug. Papers are scattered all over the room, and my suitcases have been tossed.

Blood roars in my ears as I rush into the bathroom, but it's empty. There's no sign of Jericho anywhere.

Where is he? I'm screaming on the inside, but no words come out of my mouth.

I run back to the door, my lungs burning and my stomach dropping to my feet as I bolt down the hall. I jab the elevator button and charge toward the doors as they open.

But it's not empty.

Belevich is inside.

"You left before you could collect the rest of your winnings."

Belevich narrows his gaze on me as I stumble back until my shoulder blades hit the opposite wall, swinging my head back and forth as I look around for any kind of weapon. But there's nothing. Not even a fucking vase.

"What the fuck is wrong with you?" His expression morphs into one of confusion.

"Get away from me. Get the fuck away from me right now."

The elevator doors begin to close, but Belevich stops them with a hand. He steps out, his attention catching on the oversized check I dropped as soon as I stepped out of the elevator.

"What happened?"

"Did they do this? *Did your people do this?*" My voice comes out as a ragged scream, and Belevich looks at me like I've lost my goddamned mind.

"Do what?"

I point down the hall. "Kill them . . ." My voice breaks before I can finish saying the words. "And take my husband."

Indy and Jericho's story will conclude in the final book of the Forge trilogy, *Heart of the Devil*.

ALSO BY MEGHAN MARCH

FORGE TRILOGY:

Deal with the Devil

Luck of the Devil

Heart of the Devil

SIN TRILOGY:

Richer Than Sin

Guilty as Sin

Reveling in Sin

MOUNT TRILOGY:

Ruthless King

Defiant Queen

Sinful Empire

SAVAGE TRILOGY:

Savage Prince

Iron Princess

Rogue Royalty

BENEATH SERIES:

Beneath This Mask

Beneath This Ink

Beneath These Chains

Beneath These Scars

Beneath These Lies

Beneath These Shadows

Beneath The Truth

ABOUT THE AUTHOR

Meghan March has been known to wear camo face paint and tromp around in the woods wearing mud-covered boots, all while sporting a perfect manicure. She's also impulsive, easily entertained, and absolutely unapologetic about the fact that she loves to read and write smut.

Her past lives include slinging auto parts, selling lingerie, making custom jewelry, and practicing corporate law. Writing books about dirty-talking alpha males and the strong, sassy women who bring them to their knees is by far the most fabulous job she's ever had.

She would love to hear from you, connect with her at:

Website: meghanmarch.com
Facebook: /meghanmarchauthor
Twitter: @meghan_march
Instagram: @meghanmarch

Made in the USA
Coppell, TX
03 April 2021

53033368R10163